He led her
down the garden path . . .

"Do you remember those evenings at the pond," he asked softly, "when we would go swimming under the stars?"

Samantha was taken aback. What had possessed him to bring that up? She blushed at the thought of how skimpy were the garments in which they swam. It was nothing to them then, of course. They were just children, and these strange undercurrents that now flared between them had not been present then.

Their evening swim had been one of those secret, magical rituals of childhood . . . Until one summer Edward did not come to the pond. The hurt, a child's hurt, had been devastating. They had never discussed it.

"You stopped coming."

He took her hand and rubbed it between his. The warmth traveled up her arm and down into the pit of her stomach.

"Yes," he said, fixing her with a steady gaze. "Childhood does not last forever . . ."

PRAISE FOR *WORDS OF LOVE*:

"Connoisseurs of superior Regency romance will relish this delicious comedy of manners from the pen of one of the genre's brightest new stars."

—*Romantic Times*

Jove titles by Eileen Winwood

NOBLE DECEPTION
WORDS OF LOVE

Words of Love
Eileen Winwood

JOVE BOOKS, NEW YORK

WORDS OF LOVE

A Jove Book / published by arrangement with
the author

PRINTING HISTORY
Jove edition / September 1992

ISBN: 0-515-10928-2

Jove Books are published by The Berkley Publishing Group,
200 Madison Avenue, New York, New York 10016.
The name ''JOVE'' and the ''J'' logo
are trademarks belonging to Jove Publications, Inc.

10 9 8 7 6 5 4 3 2 1

For Tricia, and secrets

Chapter 1

Sussex, 1816

"Now here is a promising notice, Edward! A 'gentlelady' in Marylebone Street seeks 'similar person of good character to serve as companion.' That is just the sort of thing I would be quite good at, you know. And I have always fancied town ways. Perhaps I ought to send a letter forthwith!"

A noisy rustling of the newspaper was the only response. The young lady, evidently expecting little else, did not allow her companion's obvious lack of enthusiasm to dampen her own and continued her monologue.

"It might answer very well, for I cannot count on having a successful Season, although your mother is all that is kind, of course. To be honest, I do not believe I should take." She wrinkled her freckled nose and sighed audibly. "Men simply do not cluster around me as they do Cecelia. It wouldn't bother me at all if there were not this great necessity at the moment of finding a husband!"

Almost imperceptibly the newspaper lowered a bit, exposing a shock of tousled blond hair and affording the veriest glimpse of a pair of cobalt eyes. They looked at the young lady for a quick moment and then resumed a studied perusal of the *Times*.

"I cannot blame Papa for leaving us without a feather to

fly with,'' she continued. ''He did care for us, to be sure. It is just that he had . . . other interests.''

A sharp crackling of the paper nearly made her jump out of her chair. The cobalt eyes glanced up with utter disdain, and a lazy baritone filled the momentary silence.

''Too much bark on it, Sam, even for you. Your papa was a flat if ever there was one. He should have had the sense to stop before he was cleaned out.'' The blue eyes disappeared again behind the newspaper with an air of finality.

The young lady so addressed looked at the gentleman in disgust and tossed her chestnut hair, which was rebelling as usual from the ribbon that bound it.

Miss Samantha Compton was accounted no great beauty, except for the hazel eyes with the intriguing flecks of gold that occasionally flickered with the unawakened promise of long-banked fires. Just now, those eyes were flashing an angry glare that, had her companion seen it, might have given even him pause.

As she had known Edward Harrowby, earl of Landsdown, for most of her one and twenty years—indeed, counted him as the brother she never had—Miss Compton was in no way loath to give him a piece of her mind.

''It is too bad of you, Edward, to criticize Papa so! I know he was not quite the upstanding fellow that your papa was, but it does not stop me from missing him!'' Other ladies might have punctuated such a remark with tears and sniffles, but Samantha merely jutted out her chin as befit her stubborn and determined nature.

The earl lowered his paper to fix her with a look that on another man's features might have signified concern. Since the earl of Landsdown was known to abhor the expression of anything approaching emotion, however, few in his circle might have taken it as such.

''Come off your horses, Sam. I never meant to disparage Sir Harry. But even you must acknowledge that he left you and your mother in a bit of a fix, what with the estate—what is left of it—going to that cousin in America.''

Mollified by what might have passed as an apology, Samantha nodded.

"And Mama is not really in any condition to launch me, so it falls to the countess. But we must quit Comptonwood by autumn in any event, Edward, and I cannot like the odds of finding a husband this spring. Any man is bound to think me a bluestocking at the outset. You know I am not in the ordinary way, in looks or conversation. And if anyone found out the whole of it, my ship would truly be sunk!"

Edward shifted his position slightly, stretching out his long legs in Sir Harry's sunny morning room, which the earl had claimed as his domain throughout the years that he and his sister, Cecelia, had run tame at Comptonwood.

"In that I fear you are correct, my dear," he readily agreed, idly brushing the sleeve of his blue kerseymere morning coat. Then he gave her a look of mock horror. "None of my set would knowingly take a bride who *writes*. Egad!"

"The more I hear of your set, the less eager I am to cast my fate before their elegantly groomed personages," Samantha muttered.

Then she continued in a determined voice. "I shall not give up my books, Edward, even if it means I must forego a husband and take a post as a lady's companion, for those books are my greatest pleasure!"

Her declaration elicited a scornful smile.

"They are fluff and nonsense for ladies' daydreams, Sam. All those tales of matchmaking and romance—I wonder where you get all those notions."

"You may call it nonsense because I well know that *you* have never had a romantic notion in your life, Edward Harrowby! But I daresay the rest of the world is not so bereft. Let us not discuss Mrs. Radcliffe, for I can see you would disdain the work of a mere woman! But what of Mr. Walpole? Never say that preoccupation with 'fluff and nonsense' led *that* gentleman to write *Otranto*!"

"Ghastly tale . . ." he murmured.

"Ghostly, perhaps," she retorted, "but romantic for all that, although I suppose one *might* wish that death had not intervened to so thoroughly thwart matters between the young lovers."

"Indeed," Edward agreed, the single word laced with sarcasm.

"Still, such an accomplished work by a man virtually *steeped* in politics and the finer arts must press even such a cynic as you, Edward, to acknowledge its worth!"

Samantha leaned back in her chair, crossing her arms with a challenging grin. But Edward simply arched a brow and glanced out the window with an air of supreme boredom.

"I daresay he was merely driven to distraction by politics," he responded, and yawned.

"You are insufferable," Samantha snapped, but her mouth curved in a smile.

At that, Edward put a quizzing glass to his eye and fixed her with a withering stare. Samantha beheld his fish eye and burst into laughter.

"An excellent imitation of Brummell, I don't doubt."

"Not these days, I fear, for his stock has greatly fallen, as you would know if you weren't such a creature of the country," was the offhand reply, uttered as the speaker delicately buffed his immaculate nails on his coat sleeve and then subjected them to elaborate inspection.

Samantha shot him a good-humored smile.

"I bow, sir, to your superior knowledge of London. But I do know that *your* stock is as elevated as ever it has been. And I would give my dowry to see the simpering misses at Almack's quail for fear of having displeased the rich and fastidious Landsdown!"

He raised his glass again, and Samantha giggled merrily.

"You really are a brute, Edward, with all your airs. Doing it much too brown, but I vow I cannot seem to stop laughing."

Far from being offended, the earl allowed one of his rare smiles to cross his face.

"'Tis well I am not bothered by your poor opinion of me, Sam. Otherwise I would spend my days in the doldrums. Only think what might happen if the rest of the world were cast into peals of laughter every time I attempted a devastating setdown."

Samantha waved her hand in dismissal.

"Pooh! Your reputation is safe with me! It is only that I have known you forever and don't blink an eye at your supercilious ways. But, Edward, we were speaking of my books."

"Ah, yes. The 'fluff and nonsense.'"

"My books are in demand, you know. Or rather I should say Mrs. Wellesly's are, for it would not do to let it be known that I am she. I'll have you know Mr. Martinsby has had no trouble selling them this year and more! It is true that there is little money in it, but it has helped Mama and me keep the wolf from the door."

Edward carefully flicked a speck of lint from his impeccably cut lapel, seemingly lost for a moment in reflection; but of course with his lordship it was impossible to know for certain.

A gentleman of superb but remote bearing, the earl of Landsdown was invariably attired as befit the bow window set, though he had never admired that rather poisonous group. Nevertheless, he had, in his own way in recent years, become one of society's most elegant specimens.

Despite Samantha's comments, however, he was not one who prized his appearance to the exclusion of all other concerns. Rather, he simply carried his long frame with an air of easy authority, his languid comportment proclaiming his breeding more than any of the fops and frills affected by the dandy set. His golden blond hair was effortlessly arranged in a careless style that some envious bachelors yearned to accomplish. His tailoring was superior in all ways, but he was never so gauche as to drop the name of his Bond Street artist at the least invitation. Such inquiries, in fact, were met by a questioning arch of the brow, an unspoken suggestion that anyone who need ask was perhaps still an apprentice in the art of sartorial excellence.

His disposition was pleasant enough, at least until the earl was crossed, when an icy look or chilling word was usually sufficient to deal with the matter. For Lord Landsdown was a physically intimidating man, although he was not especially broad of shoulder or girth. Rather, he possessed the lean, sinewy build of an acrobat, an athlete at the peak of his form. As indeed, at the age of twenty-six, he was.

Whether Samantha was correct in her assessment about his lack of interest in romantic matters would be difficult to say. Certainly none of the earl's friends had known him to favor any particular lady, although he was sometimes seen in the company of an eligible miss or two. More often, his female companions ran to the fashionably impure, and none of them had ever succeeded in capturing his affections. One fact was certain: no one had ever known the earl to be moved to a passionate display of any sort. His heart was in a fair way to being considered impenetrable.

On this occasion a tightening of the corners of his mouth was the only outward sign of his reaction to Samantha's statement.

"You know you need never fear the wolf at the door, Sam. I am losing patience with this harangue. My mother is your godmama, after all. You know we will provide for you."

"I do not want your charity, Edward!" Samantha retorted, and then had the grace to feel guilty as she heard her words.

"To be sure, your mama is generous beyond everything to offer to launch me this Season," she added hastily. "But you must see that does not answer for the future. I shall not take, and that is that. What is to happen afterward? I must look to my own resources to provide for Mama and me."

The earl picked up his newspaper again and rattled it impatiently.

"Well, you will not find the answer in the Wanted Notices. You would never survive as companion to some old biddy. Your spirit would rebel against such a dull existence in a matter of weeks."

Samantha considered that.

"Well, then," she said, turning again to the notices, "mayhap I should be searching for a different type of advertisement. This gentleman, for example, declares outright his need for a bride! And he promises 'if the lady is not naturally vicious, to study by every means in his power to promote domestic felicity'!''

Her eyes brimmed with tears of mirth.

''I declare I am tempted, Edward. It would save everyone the considerable expense of a Season!''

''And make your life thoroughly miserable,'' he snapped disdainfully.

Her eyes had taken on a faraway look, and her generous mouth curved in a half smile. Seeing her face, the earl gave a derisive snort.

''Daydreaming won't pay the piper, Sam.''

''Nonsense! Mr. Walpole was a great dreamer, you know. But I was just thinking, Edward, that if only something untoward would happen to me as it does to my characters. You know, an abduction by a handsome stranger . . .''

''Like the kidnapping you devised in your last book, I suppose. But it don't do to snatch young ladies these days, Sam. Bad *ton*.''

Samantha frowned and then shook her head.

''You may ridicule me as you like. But I would find it most romantic to meet a dashing highwayman as my Regina did!''

The cobalt eyes filled with scornful disbelief, but Edward said nothing, and his face quickly became unreadable as she continued.

''Dark, yes, he must be dark like my Lord Raven in *Love Marches to Falmouth*. Dark heroes are most out of the ordinary way,'' Samantha said. ''I can see his raven-black hair and dark eyes now. He was a bit of a rake, to be sure, but eminently reformable. Of course, he would come when I least expected it to rescue Mama and me from penury. Perhaps he would not notice that I am not a great beauty.''

Hearing the wistful note in her voice, she laughed abruptly, shaking her head.

''I am full of nonsense, Edward, as I am sure you are but waiting to point out. Still, it is pleasant to dream a bit.''

Lord Landsdown's mouth pulled almost imperceptibly into what might have been a smirk. He casually raked a hand through his blond locks and disappeared behind his paper, leaving Samantha to her own thoughts.

She found herself staring out the window for a long time, retreating into the companionable silence between friends. Despite her fanciful notions, she was in fact a sensible young lady. She knew she could not rely on her fantasies, nor did she intend to leave off her practical planning for the future in the frivolous hope that her salvation would come galloping up on a white charger. No, she would have to manage to find a husband, preferably a wealthy one, and he undoubtedly would not be the dashing hero of her dreams. But try as she might, she could not envision the man who would want her for his bride.

Samantha's absorption in her thoughts was such that she was completely unaware of the cobalt eyes that surreptitiously studied her over the top of the newspaper.

Chapter 2

"I beg your pardon, Mama. Do forgive me for not attending." Samantha looked solicitously at the delicate figure enshrouded in pale blue satin and a frilly overgown of blue netting.

The lady reclining on the divan emitted a long-suffering sigh accompanied by a look of practiced stoicism. Clarissa Compton had been an invalid for years, since her discovery that she was no match for the volcanic and spendthrift baronet she had married. Finding it impossible to defy him and not liking to cower openly in the face of his mercurial nature and tendency to dismiss all opposition as prittle prattle, Lady Compton had, quite simply, taken herself to bed. And there she had remained. Her husband's death nearly two years ago, unwisely attempting a fence in a neck-or-nothing race while in his cups, had somehow not provided the impetus to alter what had become an altogether comfortable state.

"I wish, Samantha, that you would give me your attention just this once," Lady Compton admonished. "For although I know Amanda will give you the best of counsel, it is a mother's duty not to send her only daughter off into the world without any notion of how to go on."

Samantha smiled and reached down to give her mother a hug.

"Nonsense, Mama! You are not sending me off into the world. I am but going to London for the Season with Edward, Cecelia, and Lady Landsdown! We will attend routs and balls, and I shall look for a husband. What harm can come of that?"

Lady Compton did not reply, remembering her own come-out with Amanda Huntley and the heady Season in which the two best friends were the talk of the *ton*. Amanda had chosen well, finding herself the rich Landsdown, who was as generous in spirit as he was plump of purse. But Clarissa had been so mesmerized by Harry's glittering brown eyes and commanding figure that she refused to listen to her own papa's warning about the baronet's tendency to run in dun territory. As the years passed, she had had occasion to regret her choice as she discovered that she was not up to the challenge of Harry's strong will. Amanda, she knew with a certainty not entirely born of charity, would have pulled him into line, as indeed she had excelled in so many other areas.

Forcing her attention to the matter at hand, Lady Compton surveyed the young lady who stood before her. She was by no means disappointed in what she saw, although it was quite obvious that Samantha had more of Sir Harry in her makeup than her mother perhaps would have wished. Samantha possessed Lady Compton's own slender build, a trait that in the mother had developed into a frailness of constitution; but Samantha's lean frame radiated the strong good health of a high-strung and superbly conditioned filly. Lady Compton shuddered at such an inelegant comparison, although she knew it for a particularly apt one. Her daughter was forever plunging off into the countryside on long walks or racing hell-for-leather with Edward on that bounding nag she called Captain. Amanda would have her hands full if she meant to turn the spirited Samantha into a prize on the marriage mart.

Lady Compton allowed a faint smile to cross her face. Her daughter had indeed inherited the best of Harry, the side of him that had drawn her into his arms over two decades ago. Samantha possessed his exuberance, strength, and determination. Moreover, her exposure to the straitened circumstances into which his gambling had brought them had given her a disgust of the high life, so there was no danger Samantha would be drawn into that insidious pit.

Still, Lady Compton was worried. Although Samantha was a practical miss, having long since taken over the management of the household, she had seen little of the world. Even now, on the verge of a belated London Season, she seemed much younger than her years. She had a disturbing tendency to daydream and to spend long hours in her room writing in what she insisted was a private journal. Lady Compton frowned. There was a secretive side to Samantha, and it gave her the headache to contemplate what she might be up to.

"You will promise me, Samantha, to abide by your godmother's wishes in all things. I do not wish you to go off on your own or undertake any of your pranks with Edward."

"I do not think you need worry about Edward being a disrupting influence, Mama. He has taken on such airs since he came into the title! Sometimes I think I do not know him at all. If I suggest anything untoward, he simply looks at me as if I had two heads! Not that I would do anything unseemly, to be sure," Samantha added hastily, remembering Edward's horrified initial reaction last year when she told him about her books.

Lady Compton put a pale hand to her head, which was beginning to throb in earnest. Her lashes fluttered, and her limpid blue eyes closed for a moment. Samantha was right about Edward, who had turned into such a pattern card of propriety that Lady Compton no longer recognized the boy whose devilish spirit had easily matched Samantha's. Harry had been forever pulling them out of one scrape or another. Although Edward was older than Samantha, his resolute efforts as a youth to put his boyhood behind him had been constantly foiled by Samantha's mischievous pranks. Lady Compton suspected he still had a spark or two of the scamp inside him waiting to be ignited. And if anyone could do that, she knew, it surely was Samantha.

Lady Compton opened her eyes to study her daughter, but she saw only a guileless face with a slightly upturned nose, framed by thick chestnut hair. Her daughter's hazel eyes were returning her look with unblinking calmness.

"Do not worry about me, Mama. Take care of yourself. I shall write every day!" The words were delivered with robust cheer, though to a mother's discerning ear they sounded forced. Samantha gave her a bracing hug.

Lady Compton saw the resolution in her daughter's eyes. She put her hand to her temple at the blinding stab of pain that signaled the beginning of yet another headache.

"Astley's. I must see Astley's! There is to be ropedancing and clowns and— Listen, Edward! It says here that Miss Bannister will 'execute various pleasing performances never yet attempted by any person but herself'! Oh, and Drury Lane has *Macbeth* with Mr. Kemble *and* Mrs. Siddons! 'Tis a benefit to mark their first reunion on the stage since her retirement!"

Samantha eyed the newspaper with a rapt look that normally signaled her first glimpse each spring of Captain's newest offspring. She was dressed in a sprigged muslin that was not, perhaps, of the first stare, but that did not hinder her enthusiasm as her eyes raced over the pages of the *Times* on this her first morning in London. She tossed her hair and glanced up with the eagerness of a small child.

Edward looked across his breakfast table at Samantha's dancing eyes and infectious smile. But his brows knit together, and his voice held a note of bored sophistication.

"If every meal is to be cut up in this manner by your childish exuberance, Sam, perhaps it would be a kindness for all of us if you would consider taking a tray in your room." With that, he returned to the task of completing his breakfast.

Lady Landsdown looked over at her son and wondered, not for the first time, how she had managed to produce such a stickler. Despite her good fortune to have married into a family of the finest standing, Amanda Huntley had always been something of a free spirit. She had married for love, not for a title, and for that she had always been thankful. Although Spenser had been gone nearly three years, she would ever cherish the time they had had. She sighed. It was too bad that Clarissa had not been so fortunate in her marriage. And if Clarissa persisted in keeping to her bed, well, there was nothing to be done about that. But at least, Lady Landsdown thought, she could remedy Samantha's situation. Her goddaughter was as dear to her as her own children, and it was Lady Landsdown's fondest wish to see Samantha happily settled. Unfortunately Samantha's situation was, while not completely desperate, rather urgent. With only a small dowry and no income, it was imperative that Samantha find a husband this Season. Indeed, there was no reason for Edward to try to dampen Samantha's spirits. Circumstances alone could do that, if her hosts did not have a care.

Lady Landsdown weighed taking her son to task for his remarks, but she considered it likely that Samantha would undertake that, as indeed that young lady did.

"Oh, stubble it, Edward! Well I know that a man of your consequence would be greatly embarrassed to let it be known among your town set that you must escort such a green girl as I. But I will not allow you to blacken my spirits, and so if anyone is to leave the breakfast table, I'll warrant it shall be you!"

Petersham, Lord Landsdown's butler, in the process of directing a footman to clear the table, had reason to thank his long years of service for the fact that he did not gasp aloud in horror at Miss Samantha's remarks, notwithstanding the long familiarity between the two families. The hapless footman, however, was not so fortunate and took that moment to drop a plate of ham onto the floor, splattering his lordship's well-polished boots.

Edward directed an eloquently stony glare at the quaking servant before returning his attention to Samantha.

"I take leave to point out that it is my table you so imperiously ordered me to quit," he said haughtily. "And if you are to go on in society, may I suggest that you leave off such expressions as 'stubble it'?"

Lady Landsdown coughed delicately into her napkin as Samantha glared at Edward and opened her mouth to reply.

"Now, now," the countess admonished quickly. "Let us have some harmony at table." Lowering her voice, she added: "Sam, Edward is quite right that such expressions are not quite the thing. But if both of you plan to conduct yourselves in this manner the entire Season, I daresay *I* shall take breakfast in my room, for this is quite like living with two quarrelsome children."

Samantha blushed and quickly rose to embrace the countess.

"You are quite right, ma'am. I apologize for my ungrateful temper. Edward and I shall henceforth inconvenience only ourselves with our quarrels." Samantha looked over at Edward, who was staring churlishly at a plate of kidneys. "If you will excuse me, my lady, I will prepare for our shopping expedition."

With that, Samantha quit the room, leaving Lady Landsdown to ponder her son's behavior. When the servants had left as well, the countess addressed him.

"I cannot like your treatment of Samantha, Edward. She is our guest, after all, and I know I need not remind you how important this Season is for her future."

At her quiet words, Edward looked up. His face was now impassive, although there was perhaps a slight furrow to his brow. After a moment he spoke in a toneless voice.

"I shall apologize at the first opportunity."

He hesitated and then continued with perhaps a bit more warmth. "Do you think it is wise to plunge Sam so precipitately into the whirlwind of the Season? She is, by her own admission, a green girl. I would not want her head turned by some circumstance she had not anticipated."

Lady Landsdown stared at her son in consternation. He was a handsome figure, she acknowledged, and his fortune and address had made him a sought-after prize for London hostesses, eager young misses, and their mamas. He moved in the highest circles and well knew the ways of the *ton*. And despite their spats, he knew Samantha well, perhaps better than anyone else. If he were concerned about a possible misstep on her part, perhaps he had reason to be. But the countess shook her head. Samantha Compton was a young lady of eminent good sense. If she lacked town polish, well, that could be remedied in short order. In fact, they were about to begin the process this very morning with a trip to the modiste. Lady Landsdown rose decisively.

"I have every confidence in Samantha, Edward, and I know she will conduct herself as befits her breeding and intelligence. Moreover, we are here to guide her. Your concern does you credit. But may I remind you that we are about the business of finding her a suitable husband? That should be our overriding concern. I know I can count on you to see that we do not fail."

Lady Landsdown quit the room, leaving her son staring fixedly at his tarnished boots.

Chapter 3

Samantha sealed the letter to her mother. It was a gay missive, betraying none of the doubts she had about the future. In truth, Samantha had not had to force the air of enthusiasm that had crept into the note, as it had quite swept her away from the moment she arrived at the door of Number 10 Charles Street.

The house just off Berkeley Square exuded all the splendor that the seven previous earls of Landsdown and their burgeoning fortunes could ensure. Its dark gray stone façade occupied a goodly portion of the block and stood in elegant contrast to the smaller three-story brick houses that lined much of the street. The stately stone, however, enabled the mansion to blend into its surroundings in an understated manner precisely in keeping with the tastes of the family now in residence. Large, rectangular mullioned windows viewed the sedate little street with unblinking serenity, offering mute commentary on the carriages that passed by with increasing frequency now that the winter chill had lost some of its bite.

Samantha had rarely been to London, owing to her particular family circumstances; moreover, she had never had the occasion to visit the house on Charles Street. Thus

when she had emerged from the Landsdown carriage and
peered up through iron railing at the imposing structure and
the large bronze knocker, she was quite overwhelmed.
Inside the house, her black kid half boots were outlined on
the white marble floor as she paused to behold an enormous
oak stairway that wound majestically upward, curving
gently with the stately grace of a royal antelope. The foyer
opened onto a larger adjoining hall that served upon
occasion as a ballroom. An oaken balcony ran its length,
and the walls were adorned with gold-framed portraits of
generations of Landsdowns and assorted relatives. Marble
fireplaces anchored either end of the room, and three large
chandeliers were suspended from the carved, domed ceiling.

Samantha had to shake herself to remember that she did
not really belong in this setting and that the elegant
surroundings were hers only temporarily. But when she saw
her room, she could only gaze in amazement, for it was
quite the prettiest she had ever beheld. The walls were
covered in a delightful blue, yellow, and green chintz that
propelled her into a garden of floral delights. The bedstead
had a canopy of blue and white darnix with gilt knobs and
blue and white fringe. The windows overlooked a small
garden and cobblestone courtyard. As the family was
accustomed to the latest conveniences, Samantha was not
surprised to see a water closet in the adjacent dressing room,
although she found the washstand with fitted bowl, lead
tank, and tap quite remarkable. But she was most fascinated
by the double set of brass letterboxes in the door: one to
push letters in, and the other to push them out.

She pushed out the letter to her mother and sighed. She
must not let her head be turned by it all, as that would make
it all the more difficult when the Season ended with no
husband in sight. Still, she had promised her mother to give
it a try, and so she would. And with her godmother's guidance,
who was to say she might not come about after all?

As she picked up her pelisse, Samantha paused at the
doorway. If only Edward had not been such a bear! It would
not do to be constantly at fisticuffs, not only because he was
the head of the family, but also because he was her dearest
friend.

She smiled. Through the lonely years at Comptonwood, when her mother had taken herself to bed and her father had taken himself to the gambling dens of town, Edward Harrowby had been her stalwart chum and confidant. To be sure, she knew he had sometimes found his little shadow a bit tiresome. He was, after all, almost six years her senior. When the time had come for Eton and then Oxford, the boy seemed to vanish in the ardent pursuit of manhood. And a most attractive man he had become, she thought idly, wondering what had put that thought into her head. On holidays home, he was customarily a bit stiff under the mantle of newfound maturity until she could get him to put off his airs and start being Edward again. They had quarreled over the years, much as siblings did, and neither held any regard for pretense in dealing with the other.

That thought reminded her of the morning's spat, and she squared her shoulders. She would apologize before she and Lady Landsdown undertook their shopping excursion. As she descended the stairs, she frowned. Edward had been more and more on his high ropes recently, and she wondered if it had aught to do with the plans for her Season. He seemed determined to play the role of proper guardian to her country miss. Samantha sighed in exasperation. It was true she had spent her life in the country, but that did not mean she was a complete innocent! She was twenty-one, for all that, and would have made her come-out ages ago had it not been for poor Papa's unfortunate demise. As for the rest of it, well, she had always devoured town gossip—Sussex was not so far away, after all—as well as the latest copies of *La Belle Assemblée,* the *Times*, and the *Gazette*. In her opinion, London was only bigger and more crowded than home, although certainly there were more parties and apparently a few more rules that governed one's behavior.

With that bolstering thought, Samantha found herself quite in charity with the day again as she made her way down the great staircase. Rays of sunlight streamed through the foyer windows, and her face broke into an answering sunny smile.

That is how Edward found her when he emerged into the

hall from his study, although he was forced to swerve abruptly when she suddenly turned, preoccupied, to walk in his direction. In this maneuver he was not altogether successful. For she walked squarely into him and nearly toppled them both into an enormous Chinese vase that stood nearby. As Edward reached out to steady the treasure, Samantha lost her balance and frantically clasped her arms around his middle. The awkward pas de deux ended with both parties sprawled unceremoniously on the floor, Samantha's chin resting firmly on Edward's midsection.

"Oh, I do beg your pardon, Edward! How clumsy of me! I was just coming to find you. How fortunate I am that you have not yet gone out!" Samantha turned her smiling face up to his and clasped his arm as he helped her up. "May we go into your study?"

There was a moment of silence as Edward endeavored to regain a portion of his equanimity and dignity.

"I suppose it would make no difference if I had other plans," he said at last, his voice heavy with sarcasm as Samantha half pulled him along the corridor. "My dear, you really must strive for a bit more indirectness of approach if we are to succeed at making you the Season's success."

But Samantha heard the hint of a smile in his voice and turned to him with an impish grin as they reached the study.

"You shall not provoke me, Edward! I am sure your part in our collision was at least as great as mine. It is merely that the great Landsdown will not admit to anything as inelegant as a want of balance," Samantha said as she spun gaily around and sat in a chair in front of him. "At all events, I came to offer my apologies for behaving like a child this morning. I do not wish us to quarrel, and if it will help, I will try to curb my unruly ways. Though I do not know if I can quite contain my enthusiasm, for this is quite the most exciting of times!"

She paused, then added shyly, "Ought we not to breakfast together, after all? I would *so* miss your company."

Edward stared down at the dancing hazel eyes and felt his temper cool. He studied the face cocked expectantly to one side and saw the little scamp who had followed him around for most of his youth, teasing and provoking him until the great loneliness that enveloped her lifted for a time.

His face relaxed, and his eyes took on a distant look.

"Do you remember the time Squire Walmsley's hounds treed you along with that cursed fox?"

Samantha was momentarily at a loss. Then her brow cleared.

"Oh, to be sure. When I was eight! Poor Squire, his hunt was quite ruined when you swept in on that rackety old bay to cast pepper down on the lot of them!" Samantha laughed merrily. "It was quite the most dashing rescue I have ever had!"

"Well, you ought not be so proud of it. Rum foolish to have taken the fox up like that. You could have been torn to shreds by those blasted hounds!"

Edward rubbed his chin and forced his eyes to focus on the chestnut head before him.

"I don't know what made me think of that just now."

Samantha regarded him thoughtfully. Unexpectedly she rose and moved to touch his arm.

"I do, goose! You are thinking that you may well have to rescue me all over again, this time from social disaster!" She smiled. "But I promise you, Edward, I will put my unacceptable cant and ways aside and be a pattern card of propriety while I am on the marriage mart."

She stood on tiptoe to brush his cheek with a sisterly kiss.

"Who knows, I might even find a husband to take me off your hands," Samantha said affectionately. She moved toward the door, missing the sudden rigidity that transformed Edward's features.

As she grasped the door handle, she whirled around. "Now, may we cry friends?" she said, smiling. "Although I don't recall your bothering to apologize, now that I think on it."

After a barely perceptible pause, Edward's face lightened.

"Did I not? 'Tis more than you deserve, you know. But in the spirit of peace, I do most humbly beg your pardon, my dear Sam, for behaving like the brute you are always accusing me of being.''

"You are only a brute when you wish to be, Edward. And sometimes you can actually manage something approximating charm. 'Tis fortunate you do not waste it on me! But I know the ladies of the *ton* must swoon at Landsdown's feet whenever you exert such charm on them!''

Samantha swept gaily from the study, her laughter trickling back over her shoulder and settling about Edward like a mantle of stone.

"Oh, Samantha! Edward is to take us for ices at Mr. Gunter's, and then we are to join Mama for our first outing in the park! Mama says you are to wear the new forest green, as it will set off your complexion and hair. I shall wear my new cream—the blue trim matches my eyes, don't you know? Oh, hurry, or we shall be late, and you know how Edward does insist on promptness!''

During this breathless monologue, Samantha had quietly slipped some papers on which she was writing into a drawer of her writing table. It was too bad to be interrupted just as she was beginning to get the outlines of her hero's character. But the outing sounded delightful, and she was eager for her first exposure to the afternoon ritual in the park. She smiled as she regarded the animated figure before her.

At eighteen Lady Cecelia Harrowby was in the first blush of a certain beauty that only increases with the years. She was fair, but not in the insipid style of some of the reigning debutantes; for her lashes were dark, framing a pair of sparkling eyes that had departed from the steely Landsdown cobalt of her brother and found their own startling shade of purest azure. Her figure was petite and her demeanor so demure as to invoke in the masculine heart a compelling urge to defend such a fragile treasure to the death. It was only the eyes that betrayed her. Lady Cecelia was no fragile flower for the picking—and any gentleman who took the trouble to gaze beyond the blond curls, upturned nose, and perfectly formed figure might have seen in those penetrating blue eyes a lively intelligence and strength of will.

Samantha knew she would be quite cast in the shade by the lovely Lady Cecelia. It did not, however, bother her one whit. She loved Cecelia as a sister and wished her the joy of the hugely successful Season she would undoubtedly have. It was true that Samantha spared a small thought for the hope that not all masculine eyes would be riveted on her beautiful friend when the two of them were together. When she reflected further upon the matter, however, Samantha knew she would rather find a husband who would not be so blinded by the sun as to miss the moon. She frowned. Somehow, the comparison was not quite right, but perhaps she could improve on it and work it into her current manuscript.

"Oh, do quit woolgathering, Sam! Have you not heard a word I have said?"

The words caught her wandering thoughts, and Samantha again looked up at the excited young lady before her.

"Of course I have, Cecelia! I am most eager for an afternoon outing. Although I am certain you shall outshine every young lady in the park! Let us be off!"

"Fustian! Did I not say you are to change? I told you Mama wishes to see you in the green muslin. And she is quite right. It will set off your hair, which I must say is much improved since yesterday's visit by Madame Christiana!"

Samantha did not take offense at the comment; indeed, the truth was ever evident when she looked into her glass. The unruly, shapeless mop had been replaced by a halo of neat curls that framed her face and seemed to bring out her eyes. Longer tresses trailed down her neck to give her a flattering and more sophisticated look that Madame Christiana insisted would set her apart from the insipid misses just out of the schoolroom.

"Thank you for that bracing compliment, dearest," Samantha said, laughing. "I shall join you shortly. Who knows—I may even claim some of your beaus."

Cecelia blushed.

"As to that, Samantha, I have no beaus yet as you well know. And you may claim them in your own right, for I have never seen you look lovelier!"

Samantha thanked her with a hug and summoned her maid to help her change. An hour later, she and Cecelia sat with Edward in an open carriage under the trees across Berkeley Square from Gunter's. Samantha sipped a white currant ice, while Cecelia relished a pineapple. Samantha was amazed to see the waiters scurrying to and fro with trays of ices as dozens of well-dressed ladies reclined in their carriages enjoying the unseasonably warm weather.

"I do not see why the waiters must come such a distance," Samantha said. "I am sure we are perfectly capable of transporting our own ices from the shop."

"Oh, but it would not be at all the thing, Samantha," Cecelia said, shocked.

"That is right, my dear," Edward added in a sardonic tone. "Bad *ton* to do such work yourself, you know."

Then he lowered his voice. "The real reason, if you must know, my country innocent, is that Gunter's business falls off dramatically once the Season ends. So he hustles to sell us all the confectionery delights he can while we are here. It is less a matter of good manners and more a matter of good business to so indulge our lazy whims."

Samantha pondered that and then turned her attention to Cecelia, who was chatting about the cake Lady Landsdown had commissioned for their ball. Samantha's thoughts wandered to the eligible gentlemen she hoped to meet. Would they be terribly formal and unapproachable, like Edward when he put on airs? She stifled a giggle.

"Edward," Cecelia was saying, "do you not think Samantha's new hairstyle most attractive? I'll wager she will draw all eyes at the park today!"

Edward glanced over at Samantha, who was in the act of tracing with her finger the path of an icy rivulet trickling down her glass.

"I agree, sister dear, although I must say Sam has a way of managing to draw all eyes whatever the circumstance," he replied, his eyebrows arching in disapproval as the subject of their conversation stuck out her tongue and whisked the trickle into her mouth with a quick but demure move.

Samantha leaned back in her seat to savor the taste and closed her eyes in delight. When she opened them, she saw Edward's mouth pursed, censure written on his face.

"I know, Edward, you find my manners wanting. But, pray, look around us. We are outdoors and not in some stuffy drawing room, after all. Must you be such a stickler?"

"Our location should have no bearing on your conduct, Sam. If you cannot control your manners with us, pray do endeavor not to embarrass my mother with such antics when we are in company."

Cecelia eyed them silently and waited for fireworks; but Edward's remark had been delivered with such exaggerated hauteur that Samantha knew it for a hum. The twinkle in his eye was all the confirmation she needed, and she gave a whoop of laughter that drew quite a few eyes to their group.

"You are doing it again, Edward, and I should box your ears. But not even you can cast me into the doldrums today, for we are going to the park, and perchance I shall meet the man of my dreams! What say you to that?"

"Only that he is welcome to you, my dear."

Samantha pulled a mock frown and then reached out to rap Edward's knuckles with her spoon. The earl pretended to be in great pain, which provoked more laughter from Samantha. Cecelia rolled her eyes at both of them and resumed her study of the extraordinary profusion of ostrich plumes on the hat of a lady in a nearby carriage.

When the earl's landau pulled into the park later that afternoon, Samantha and Cecelia were positioned opposite Lady Landsdown, while the earl rode his roan alongside. Their group created quite a sensation, as Lady Landsdown had expected.

"I am delighted that the weather cooperated with our plans, girls," she said as she spied the first group of eager gentlemen riding over to greet them. "You both do me credit today."

Lady Landsdown sat back on the seat with a self-satisfied smile, at least some of her pleasure deriving from the knowledge that she herself was in looks today. Although she was widowed these three years, Lady Landsdown was by no means ready for consignment to the dowager set. Her fair hair might have a touch of silver, but her figure was still good, if perhaps a bit fuller and softer than it once had been. The riveting Landsdown eyes had not come from her side of the family, to be sure, but her own were quite a spectacular shade of green that often drew a second or third glance, even from the younger gentlemen.

And so, Lady Landsdown presided contentedly over one set of introductions after another. It seemed that an extraordinary number of her friends' sons and members of Edward's set were eager to reestablish their acquaintance with the countess of Landsdown. It was true that the chief drawing card was undoubtedly the serenely beautiful Lady Cecelia, who had the additional attraction of being from one of the wealthiest families in London. But Lady Landsdown was happy to observe that Samantha came in for her share of interested looks, and she privately predicted a morning room full of callers tomorrow.

Samantha was trying to remember the names of the last two bucks who had claimed Edward's friendship when she suddenly spied an imposing figure mounted on a magnificent black stallion some distance away. The rider himself was attired in black. He held to the edge of the park as he surveyed in amusement the bevy of fawning bachelors around their carriage. The enormous horse pawed the ground impatiently as the man cruelly jerked the reins to hold him.

Samantha was drawn to the rider's face. Its uneven planes gave him a rough appearance that she found handsome and strangely compelling. His was not the face of a man used to spending his evenings at Almack's or in the sedate music rooms of society's hostesses. No, she suspected he had a very different idea of how to spend an evening, and an inadvertent tingle danced up her spine. His dark eyes caught hers and glittered, and he tipped his hat mockingly, exposing a head of windswept, raven-black hair. She shuddered.

Edward, trying to contain his boredom at the tedious chitchat with acquaintances he could barely recall, glanced over at Samantha. He followed her mesmerized gaze and froze.

The rider, perhaps sensing another pair of eyes directed his way, turned and observed on the earl's features a chilling expression that held both a warning and a challenge. Their eyes locked for a long moment. Then the stranger gave a jaunty flick of the reins as he returned his gaze to Samantha. Abruptly he turned his mount and vanished into a grove of trees.

Samantha stared after him.

"I do believe you will succeed in catching half the flies in London if you do not close your lovely mouth, my dear."

She looked up, preoccupied, Edward's harsh words barely filtering through her dazed state.

"That dark-haired man, Edward, on the edge of the park. Did you see him? He was mounted on a magnificent creature. Who was he?"

"No one fit for a proper introduction, Sam, so let us drop it, if you please." Edward sat back on his roan and fixed her with a stern look. Samantha leaned forward, her eyes shooting fire.

"I hope I am not such a green girl that I will allow you to judge the character of someone I have not even met!" she retorted. "I shall insist on picking my own acquaintances, Edward, and I command you to tell me the identity of that gentleman!"

The earl stiffened and when he spoke, his words exuded cold anger. "I doubt that many of the *ton* would grant him that title, although he holds many others, my foolish little tyrant. His most noteworthy skills are not fit to be discussed in polite company, if you must know, consisting chiefly of seducing innocents, appropriating fortunes, cuckolding husbands, and dueling with those so unwise as to challenge his right to do so."

A gasp signaled that Lady Landsdown had heard Edward's remarks. Cecelia's head bobbed up in alarm. Samantha simply stared at Edward, who looked away and in a supremely bored voice ordered the carriage turned in the direction of Charles Street.

Chapter 4

Lord Deverill was accustomed to the darkness and its clandestine pursuits. Indeed, it was rare for him to seek the public venue of the park during daylight, but somehow he had found himself skirting its edge this fine spring day. He was a man at the meridian of his appearance, and all who saw him could not help but be moved by the dark drama of his presence. His coal-black hair glinted in the unfamiliar sunlight, and his midnight eyes narrowed in anticipation as he surveyed the genteel scene before him. His horse, Satan, gave a snort, and Lord Deverill—"Lord Devil" to the many who feared him—pulled back on the reins.

"A moment more, Satan, and I will agree with you that it is time to be off. But hold now, for I have just seen something extraordinarily interesting."

His eyes glowed as he watched her from the edge of the park. The young lady in her carriage was surrounded by a court of eager gentlemen. She was, if not precisely beautiful, a lady of intriguing looks. Her complexion was perhaps a bit freckled—no doubt she hailed from the country. But for all that, she carried herself with distinction. Evidently she felt his eyes, for *she looked up through the crowd around her and met his gaze. Unexpectedly she gave him a luminous smile. "Odds fish, Satan. I swear I just saw the moon, although I vow it be daylight still."*

Samantha frowned. That was not quite right, but perhaps she could return to it later. She smiled and summoned the images that had remained in her since yesterday afternoon.

He must discover her name. Perhaps he could even persuade her to honor him with her company. The devil had his ways, after all. And who could tell? Perhaps she could fill the emptiness that had kept his dissolute existence from true happiness. Satan snorted, and Lord Deverill smiled. It was not really an evil smile, despite his reputation. Perhaps it was only the loneliness that made him search night after night for new pleasures. He turned his horse and vanished through a grove of trees. But not before he had seen the young lady's questioning eyes and knew they would be searching the crowd for his for a long while.

Samantha leaned back in her chair and sighed as she pondered what she had written. "The Devil Lord." It had a rather compelling ring to it. If only her life was half as exciting as her books. Her eyes drifted dreamily to the ceiling of the library, where she had retreated after being interrupted in her room a half-dozen times by Cecelia. She mulled the next scene. They would meet, perhaps at a party. Not an ordinary affair. A masquerade. Yes, that had the right touch. She picked up her pen again and soon was busily writing.

She was so intent she failed to notice the squeaking of the door; nor did she feel the eyes that studied her from the doorway.

"I suppose I must, for the duration of your stay, disabuse myself of the notion that it is possible to find peaceful sanctuary anywhere in this house."

Samantha started and then laughed as she met the familiar cobalt eyes.

"Thank goodness, 'tis only you, Edward! I have been living in dread of having to endure another of Cecelia's rapturous outbursts over the success of yesterday's drive."

She bent her head again and resumed her scribbling.

Undaunted by this unflattering reception, the earl advanced into the library.

"I suppose I must also get accustomed to these frequent setdowns." He sighed mournfully. "It is well that not all the females of my acquaintance are so enthralled with my presence, or my conceit would soon become intolerable."

As there was no response to this sally, Edward walked over to the settee on which Samantha was perched and idly perused her papers. He frowned.

"Who the devil is 'Lord Devil'?"

At this Samantha looked up, blushing furiously. She snatched the papers from his hands.

"You are not to read my work, Edward, until I say you may!" She brushed a stray lock from her face. "It is just that I haven't got him quite right, that's all, and I have no desire to display my flawed creation for all to see."

The earl arched a brow and settled his impeccably clad frame into a nearby chair.

"Ah, 'tis the muse at work again, is it not? Let me guess. 'Lord Devil' must be your latest heroic paragon of manhood. Dashing appellation, that. What does your heroine call him in their intimate moments? 'Devil,' perhaps? Charming." He crossed his arms and gave her look of bland innocence.

Samantha laughed in spite of her annoyance. She sensed that his good-humored barbs were an effort to make amends for their quarrel in the park. She decided to accept his peace offering.

"Poke fun if you like, Edward, but I warn you: if you must continue in this manner, I shall have to ask you to keep your opinions to yourself." She eyed him slyly before adding, "Although that would be a pity because I was hoping for your advice."

The earl, who had been about to immerse himself in a book, looked up quickly.

"Always at your service, of course. But something tells me this is not at all the ordinary thing. Out with it, then," he commanded with an air of resignation.

Samantha stood abruptly and walked briskly to the window. Suddenly she did not know how to begin. Nonsense, she thought, shaking her head. She had been turning to Edward for advice for years. Only this was not, well, the kind of thing they usually discussed. She whirled around.

"It is just that I can't . . . I mean I don't know how 'tis done!"

Edward, whose sense of foreboding had blossomed with this mysterious declaration, pondered the rather agitated figure of the slim woman silhouetted before the window. The useless thought idly flitted through his brain that he wished he had had the sense not to seek out his library this afternoon.

"How *what* is done? Although I rather dread your answer."

Samantha approached his chair and abruptly sat on the leather stool at his feet. She took a deep breath.

"I am glad I have you to advise me, Edward, though I feel like such a silly goose. I know you are just Edward. Still, you are a man for all that, I suppose, and this is somewhat awkward. You see . . ."

She broke off for a breathless moment before continuing in a rapid spate of words: "It is a matter of relations between ladies and gentlemen."

The earl's face had grown ever more apprehensive as this speech progressed, and he now spoke hastily to forestall what he feared would be an extremely embarrassing discussion.

"Sam, surely your mother, or if not she, then my mother, would be best to advise you. I am not at all appropriate. . . ."

"But that is just it! You are entirely appropriate!" she importuned. "And I know your experience with the ladies is *vast!* That is way you must help me!"

Here she stopped, for Edward had suddenly been overcome by a fit of coughing, and his face was quite red. She rose and began pounding him on the back.

''There, there! Whatever is wrong?'' Her own embarrassment had vanished in the face of her concern for his predicament. But Edward suddenly had himself in hand. He brushed her hands away and tried to rise from his chair.

''I am quite well, Sam, as you can see,'' he said briskly. ''Spare me your concern, and your unseemly confidences as well! I believe I recollect a pressing engagement somewhere, at all events.''

But Samantha forcefully pushed his elegant frame back into the chair.

''No, Edward, I insist you answer my questions. How else am I to know? I have no experience in these matters. And from what I can observe, many ladies are eager to have your friendship. Well, I don't mean friendship, precisely. There must be a better word for it than that. Oh, drat! You see, I am a hopeless innocent!''

She wrinkled his brow, leaned over, and fixed him with a determined gaze that seemed to Edward to bespeak anything but innocence.

''You see, I must know how it is done,'' she said firmly. ''How you attach them, I mean. How else can I write about it? I must have a gentleman's perspective. I thought if you told me how you would go about attaching a lady's interest—making love to her, you know—I could use it for my book. For I know half the ladies of the *ton* are angling for Lord Landsdown, and so there must be some secret to it all, some technique, some . . .''

Samantha stopped abruptly, as Edward's crimson face had turned even redder, and he was staring at her in utter astonishment, as if she had suddenly grown two heads. Deserted for once by his customary aplomb, the earl looked like a man completely at sea. He opened his mouth to speak and then closed it without uttering a word.

''Oh, please don't turn all proper on me, Edward!'' Samantha pleaded. ''I know this is a bit odd, well, perhaps not at all the thing, but I have no one else to turn to!''

She reached out and gently touched his arm. His eyes, fixed at a point somewhere above the top of her head, slowly dropped to hers, and an involuntary smile crept over his chiseled features.

"You, Sam, are an incorrigible scamp!"

"There, I knew you would understand!" She clapped her hands and gave a little hop-skip before turning back to him with a serious expression.

"It is all in the interest of my work, you know. Truly, I am not trying to pry into your life. Although, since you have always been so secretive about it, I can only assume that it would make for an extremely interesting discussion."

Samantha looked up expectantly, a slightly wicked grin on her face, only to be met by a pillow that seemed to come out of nowhere to glance off the side of her head.

"Oh!" she cried, as Edward was already up and attempting an exit, an unguarded expression of triumph on his face.

"I shall box your ears for that, sir!" Samantha vowed and made a very unladylike lunge for the superbly polished brown Hessians as they passed by. Her aim was sure, and Edward made an inelegant landing on the carpet. Samantha, her arms firmly clasped around the ankle of his right boot, gave a cry of glee.

"Caught! You forget, Edward, that I can move fast enough when I've a mind to. And when have you ever gotten away with such a stunt? Shame on you for even thinking to outdo me!" Her full, throaty laugh rang out, soon joined by a deeper chuckle that had been rarely heard with such abandon at Landsdown, at least since the present earl had been in residence.

Oblivious for a moment of the shocking effect of such a scene upon any casual observer, the two occupants of the room sat on the floor like giggling children, Samantha with her legs crossed under the full skirt of her morning gown and Edward ostentatiously inspecting his boots with a mock hauteur that sent Samantha into another peal of laughter. But suddenly Edward's gaze lost its luster, and he seemed to recollect his situation. With all the dignity he could muster, he lifted himself off the floor and extended a hand to help his companion up.

Samantha accepted his assistance with a look of regret.

"Oh, now I see that you are Lord Landsdown once more. Pity, I was just getting used to Edward again."

The earl bore his observation without comment, and Samantha, noting his changed mood, thought it best to effect an exit. But as she smoothed her skirts, she looked up at him.

"You will think about my request, Edward? About my book, I mean."

Edward stared at her.

"Such a discussion would be entirely inappropriate, Sam," he said quellingly. Her mutinous expression caused him to add with a sigh, "I can see you are determined to be stubborn."

She moved toward him, but he held out a hand to stop her.

"I do not intend to spend the duration of your visit being tackled in my own house and sporting bruises upon my person. We have both been out of the schoolroom for some years now, Sam. I advise you to comport yourself accordingly."

Samantha shot him an indignant look and turned to leave.

As she reached the door, she glanced back with a grin.

"I believe, my toplofty lord, that you were the one who opened fire, as it were." With that, she took the pillow that she had hidden in the folds of her dress and heaved it at him. It caromed off his chest and fell to the floor at his feet. The earl glared at her, his expression dangerous. With a merry giggle Samantha fled.

Edward surveyed the pillow ruefully and with dawning horror. It was utterly unthinkable that he had just engaged in such rough-and-tumble child's play with a young lady, who, despite their longstanding friendship, was nevertheless at the moment under his protection. What was it about Sam that made him lose all sense of propriety, all resemblance to the exceedingly correct gentleman he had worked so hard to perfect?

A sigh escaped his lips. He would be mightily glad when his mother found Samantha Compton a husband and she was his responsibility no more.

Edward settled into his chair and picked up his book. But the words blurred, and he found he could not concentrate.

Something had intruded into his peaceful existence ever
since his mother had agreed to bring Sam out, something
that had niggled at the edge of his consciousness and so
soured his disposition that he knew he had deserved his
mother's disapprobation for his demeanor at breakfast the
other day. And that something, he knew with reluctant
clarity, was the very thing he had just insisted was his
heartiest wish: a husband for Sam.

He tried without success to conjure an image of the man
he would deem appropriate for such a position. He would
have to be a man of firmness, else the little hoyden would
run circles around him. But not too firm, Edward decided,
for Sam was at heart a vulnerable innocent whose spirit
deserved to flourish in a climate of freedom and loving
patience. He smiled as he summoned the image of the little
waif he had first seen nearly fifteen years ago when he
found her curled up in the stables at Landsdown, patiently
waiting for his mother's mare, Cherub, to foal. It had been
past midnight, and he marveled that she had not been missed
at home. Later, when he became acquainted with the
situation at Comptonwood—Sir Harry's careless disregard
of his family, Lady Compton's endless illnesses, and the
servants' glaring neglect of their charge—he was not
surprised that no one had thought to keep track of the lonely
little child who was the only truly bright light in that
household.

Through the years, the little imp had tagged along in his
shadow, following him about shyly at first and then, when
she saw he tolerated her presence, more confidently. After a
while they had become fast friends as Sam adopted him as
the big brother she never had. He had delighted in the role,
protecting her and watching her spirit emerge from its shell.
She was still childlike in some ways, but she had developed
into a woman of courage and intelligence. And something
more. A woman of beauty as well. That chestnut hair was
exceptional, with highlights that danced in the firelight or
when the sun hit it in just the right way. Her eyes had an
indefinable spark that had often made him wonder just how
they would look at a man she came to love.

Abruptly he shook his head, not liking the direction in which his thoughts were meandering. Sam had indeed become an extraordinary woman, and he winced at the knowledge that they were now all about the task of marrying her off to someone who undoubtedly would not appreciate what he was getting.

Anger surged through him. He detested the marriage mart. He had had Seasons of practice in evading the eager debutantes and their mothers, beating them at their own game with his carefully cultivated superciliousness. Their desperate efforts to maneuver him into offering for some pale, vapid miss with no mind of her own had failed miserably. It was all so much hypocrisy.

But that was not the worst of it. To his view, the gentlemen were just as bad. If they were in need of blunt, they angled for the lady's dowry. If it was time to set up their nurseries, the lady's pedigree was more to the point. If they cared for neither, most likely they had only seduction in mind. At all events, they had no plans to alter their comfortable lives with their conveniently accessible mistresses.

Edward cringed at the thought of throwing Sam into such a world. She had no experience of town ways and none, certainly, of men. Her silly questions today were but one example. Teach her how a gentleman attaches a lady, indeed!

Edward allowed himself a bitter smile. He had not actually tried to ''attach'' any ladies for some time. Perhaps that is why they tended to fall at his feet. His very inaccessibility seemed to intrigue them. There was also his fortune, of course, and his sense of style that had emerged rather effortlessly after the first excesses of youth and which now seemed part of his character, part of the armor with which he faced the world.

That armor had never been pricked by any of the ladies who angled for his affections. In fact, the earl sometimes wondered why it was that he seemed to have no affections to give. It had been such a very long time since a lady had moved him, and even now that episode in his salad days caused him such embarrassment that he rarely thought on it. Since he and Lady Darrow still moved in the same circles, he had been thankful in the years since to discover that the pain of that first, passionate love had gradually eased and with it the acute embarrassment of realizing that while Catharine had been the center of his world during that brief affair, he had been to her only an amusing and youthful plaything.

Of course, Edward acknowledged with a grim smile, that had been before he had inherited the title and all its wealth. Lately, when he noticed Catharine's wandering eye upon his, he returned only a cold, stony glare that, more than anything, bespoke the cynical and protective veneer he had earnestly applied to all his emotions since that trying time.

Somehow with Sam his armor always slipped. Perhaps that was because she herself was charmingly natural, without any of the affectations that so marred the ladies of his circle.

He bent down to pick up the pillow that had so lately done battle. That episode had been more like their tiffs of old, and it had for the moment relieved some of the constraint between them that he had begun to feel of late. He did not know the cause of it, precisely, but it no doubt related to the helplessness he felt at the knowledge that her future would soon be decided. He would do all in his power to prevent her from being hurt and to see that she chose wisely. But he knew this was her only Season and her choices, of necessity, would be limited. Why did the thought of Sam walking away on some swell's arm send him into fits of gloom?

With a sigh of resignation, he placed the pillow on the settee and tried mightily to banish the image of Samantha Compton in the clutches of such unprincipled and over-weening creatures as he knew to be represented among his sex.

Chapter 5

The Landsdown town carriage was exceedingly well sprung, Samantha noted idly. To be sure, there was no reason for other than a smooth ride on this occasion, as they were only traveling a short distance to the earl of Montrose's ball in honor of his daughter, Lady Alynn. And as the streets were jammed with carriages headed in the same direction, there was no chance of going above a snail's pace. Still, Samantha observed as she settled herself comfortably amid the plush velvet cushions, there was something to be said for this mode of travel.

Edward was staring out the window with a bored expression. Lady Landsdown was smiling another of her secretive smiles that stemmed from her satisfaction with the way her charges had presented themselves for this their first ball of the Season. Clearly she was anticipating an evening of unparalleled success.

Cecelia was radiant in a pale pink gown that perfectly set off her creamy skin and shining blond hair, which curled about her face like a halo in the Grecian style. She sat quietly next to Edward, but Samantha knew that despite her silence, she, too, was filled with eager anticipation.

Samantha could not quite mask a shiver of excitement

that raced through her as she drew her shawl around her shoulders. She was wearing quite the nicest gown she had ever possessed. It was a blush peach that caught the highlights in her chestnut hair and brought out the flecks of gold in her hazel eyes. The gown itself had even drawn Edward's eye when she descended the stairs at Landsdown House. For it was no young debutante's frothy confection, but an elegant creation that emphasized the charms of the woman she had become. The ruched bodice swept low on her shoulders and fell across her breasts in a disarming manner that Madame Celeste had designed with great skill to soften Samantha's boyishly thin figure. Folds of peach silk fell in a straight line from a shimmering gold ribbon caught just under her breasts, and when Samantha moved, the folds hugged her form most attractively. A topaz pendant adorned her neck. In her hair, she wore a pale peach rose.

But other than that first look, Edward evinced no interest in the evening. In fact, he had been decidedly distant.

"Now, girls," Lady Landsdown was saying, "I have received assurances from Lady Jersey that you may waltz, although it would be a clever salute to her vanity if you were to prefer the quadrille, since she insists on credit for its introduction. You must, of course, be careful not to foster any unwanted intimacies, and prudence must surely suggest that it would not be the thing to dance *all* of the waltzes this first time. And do remember to sit out a dance or two and chat with the chaperons. That will greatly please the dowager set and cannot but contribute to your success."

Samantha frowned as she studied Edward's rigid profile. She hoped he was not still angry about this afternoon. She knew he had been shocked by her request, although the Edward of old would never have had his sensibilities offended by such a trifle. Perhaps she shouldn't have acted the hoyden by tackling him like a ill-mannered child. Her mouth pursed thoughtfully. Still, their childish antics had afforded her a glimpse of the old friend she had sorely missed in recent months. For that she could not be sorry. It was better than this infuriatingly distant coolness that he seemed to prefer in her company these days. Whatever had happened to their easy companionship?

But at the ball she found that Edward was anything but distant. In fact, he hovered about her like a protective mother hen. It was as if, Samantha thought in irritation, he feared she would embarrass him by some misstep. Every time a gentleman sought her hand for a dance, that unfortunate worthy was subjected to a chilling scrutiny and Edward's haughtiest glances. After enduring nearly an hour of such behavior, Samantha finally sought refuge in the ladies' retiring chamber. Within moments, one of the most beautiful women she had ever seen swept into the room.

The woman wore a daringly cut ice blue gown that clung to her curves as if the fabric had been dampened. Samantha shivered at the thought, as it was still rather chilly at night. The garment's neckline, outlined by delicate bands of silver beads, dipped alarmingly low over the woman's breasts. Her generous mouth had been emphasized with artificial coloring, and she had begun applying a substance to her cheeks from an enameled box when her steel gray eyes met Samantha's fascinated ones.

"You are Edward's . . . friend, of course."

The woman clearly expected no answer as she returned to her careful task. Satisfied finally, she gave her cheeks a last pinch and pulled some tendrils of blond, wispy hair loose from their restraints. She smiled at her reflection, and turned to greet Samantha with a pleasant expression.

"I am Lady Darrow. Perhaps Edward has mentioned me. No? Ah, well. You make your come-out this Season, I believe?"

Eager to show this polished lady that she was no tongue-tied miss, Samantha curtsied politely and smiled in her friendliest fashion.

"How do you do? I am Samantha Compton. And I am indeed making my come-out. But at the moment I despair of meeting any eligible gentlemen!"

At the lady's interested look, she blurted out, "You see, Edward is so afraid I will embarrass him that he is preventing me from getting to know anyone! I don't blame him, exactly, but, well, I shall never get a husband at this rate!''

An amused smile found its way across Lady Darrow's lips, although it did not, perhaps, reach her eyes.

"Poor dear! Edward can be such a beast! You must let me introduce you around. There *is* someone, as a matter of fact, who has been most interested in making your acquaintance."

With that provocative comment, the woman sailed out of the room, giving Samantha little choice but to follow.

Their appearance together at the top of the stairs leading down to the ballroom caught more than one observer's attention. From across the room, a pair of cobalt eyes stared first in disbelief, and then in patent disapproval. Much closer, at the foot of the stairs in fact, midnight eyes gazed at the ladies with a sardonic amusement that was quickly masked by a look of amiable politeness as they gracefully descended the stairway.

"Ah, Catharine, it is always a pleasure to see you, and in excellent looks, as usual. But you did not tell me you were in such delightful company tonight."

The voice, velvet smooth, brought Samantha up short, and she turned in the speaker's direction. She nearly tripped when she saw him. It was the man in the park and by the look of him, Lord Devil himself!

He was dressed all in black, save for his white shirt and the single diamond-encircled onyx pin that adorned his cravat. His unruly hair swirled about his face in a wild manner that conjured images of a windswept pirate. His penetrating eyes seemed to shoot fire, and Samantha found to her mortification that they held hers prisoner. His cheek bore a jagged scar, and his wide mouth seemed fixed in an expression that stopped just short of a sneer. His rough features were schooled into a social mask that did not, Samantha thought, look entirely natural.

She was staring, she knew, but seemed incapable of speech at the moment. It was as if her fantasy had come to life! Lady Darrow stepped into the awkward silence.

"Miss Compton, may I present Lord Blackwood? He is

an old acquaintance.'' The last two words, it seemed to Samantha, were spoken with perhaps a bit more emphasis. Smiling, Lady Darrow took Samantha's hand and gently placed it in Blackwood's.

Samantha still had not spoken. She watched, as if from a distance, as the man bowed over her hand and then turned it over to kiss her wrist. His lips sent the most delightful tingles up her arm. Goodness! Was that gasp from her own lips? Samantha shook herself back into reality. But at the precise moment when she would have reclaimed her hand, Lord Blackwood abruptly released it, and it dangled by her side like some useless appendage she had forgotten how to use.

''I believe I saw his lordship in the park earlier this week,'' Samantha said by way of acknowledging the introduction, and then wanted to bite her tongue. It would not do to show that she had been so moved by the sight of this stranger that she had preserved the memory in her brain for nearly a week!

''That is,'' she amended, ''I believe it was he, although I cannot be sure! One does not notice everyone in the park, you know.''

The marquess of Blackwood emitted a harsh laugh that sent shivers up Samantha's spine. His eyebrows arched, and his eyes bored into hers with an assessing look.

''To be sure, a lady never overplays her hand,'' he said in an enigmatic manner that brought an appreciative smile from Lady Darrow.

''Nor overstays her welcome,'' that lady added and, with a quick mocking curtsy, disappeared into the crowd.

Samantha looked around in some confusion, but the marquess had his hand lightly at her waist and was propelling her to the dance floor.

''I hope this dance is not spoken for. I would dislike having to put a period to some poor lad's existence at such a splendid occasion,'' Blackwood said.

''You do waltz?'' His words came in a silky purr.

''Yes . . .'' Samantha began haltingly. ''But as to

whether 'tis spoken for, I could not say. I must check my card. . . .''

''Pray, do not bother,'' came the insolent command, and Samantha found herself swept into a powerful set of arms that left her unable to argue and barely able to catch her breath.

She tried to keep her eyes level with the broad chest before her, but treacherously they stole up to Lord Blackwood's mesmerizing face. Her heart was beating with such force that Samantha knew he must surely feel it, and indeed his eyes wore such a knowing look that she was certain that must be the case.

This, then, was Lord Devil. A libertine, to be sure. But lonely, surely, yearning to exchange his rakish ways for love . . . Samantha broke off her thoughts as Lord Blackwood clasped her even tighter. She hoped no one noticed that he was barely observing the proprieties. She would get an earful from Edward for this, but perhaps it was worth it just for the heady experience of being in the arms of a rake. Samantha giggled. Her fantasies were spinning out of control!

Blackwood arched an eyebrow as he heard the giggle and looked down at the young lady who, he was certain, was having decidedly improper thoughts about him. He smiled. There would be time for that.

The dance swept them around the room and past one particular observer who found no amusement in watching the pair. Indeed, the earl of Landsdown's eyebrows knitted in an expression that caused his mother alarm, especially when she was the direction in which he was looking. As the music faded and Blackwood showed no sign of returning Samantha to her chaperons, Lord Landsdown's face grew even more fierce. When Blackwood and Samantha disappeared through a door leading to the garden, Lady Landsdown heard a muffled oath and looked over to see her son striding purposefully in that direction.

With a sigh the countess returned her attention to her daughter, who had returned from her own waltz with one of Edward's friends, Lord Formsby. As the latter offered to fetch the ladies a glass of negus, Lady Landsdown was constrained from setting out on her own to see what was afoot in the garden. But then, she reasoned, Edward would handle the matter with his customary poise.

The garden was alight with hundreds of tiny lanterns strung from the marble colonnade that graced the back of the large house. To Samantha it seemed as if she had entered a magical world that danced with the twinkling lights of dozens of fairies. She felt the marquess's hand as it lingered improperly at her waist and then moved her gently toward a grove of trees that was not so well illuminated. Samantha knew she should put a stop to this nonsense, but she could not still the desire to savor at least a moment of this nighttime magic.

Sighing, she opened her mouth to speak but gasped abruptly as she beheld the eyes that glinted dangerously at her, drawing her into their depths like a spider beckoning his prey ever deeper into his twisted web.

"My lord . . ." Samantha finally managed to say, but her words trailed off as Blackwood pulled her to him. Her arms went up protectively, but they were powerless against his will. His mouth came down on hers with irresistible force. She closed her eyes as his lips first teased hers and then suddenly began a bruising assault. Her brain roused itself to panic, and Samantha tried to wriggle free, but the powerful arms held her pinioned against the length of his body.

"Samantha! My mother commands your presence."

The words crackled through the garden, and suddenly the arms released her; Samantha had to put a hand out against a tree to maintain her balance.

"Well, it is the inestimable Lord Landsdown," Blackwood observed mockingly, eyes narrowing, as he nevertheless stepped away to allow greater distance between him and Samantha.

"Leave us, Samantha," Edward said, and she thought his voice held barely suppressed fury.

She looked at Edward with a dazed expression. He stood not ten feet away, resplendent in evening dress, his blond hair glinting in the twinkling glow of the lanterns. He stood at easy attention, but there was something about his lean from that gave Samantha the impression of a cat poised to strike.

"That is quite all right, Miss Compton. There is not the slightest need for you to inconvenience yourself. Although if Lady Landsdown has summoned you, to be sure you must obey," Blackwood purred. "But as it happens, I have a pressing obligation elsewhere."

Boldly he began to walk past Edward, almost daring him with his insolent silence to make a scene. To be sure, Blackwood had already calculated that Lord Landsdown was too much the gentleman for such a breach of manners at the home of one of the *ton*'s most respected families. Blackwood himself had no such qualms, but he was just as happy not to face Landsdown's wrath openly this evening. Although Blackwood was himself a noted duelist, the earl was said to be deadly at those skills as might be employed in such a match. No, Blackwood thought, he would fight his battles with more devious means. The Compton chit would wait. For a while.

Landsdown beheld Blackwood's retreating back in silence until the marquess reached the edge of the garden.

Quietly, almost like a whisper, his words reached Blackwood's ear.

"I shall kill you, Blackwood, if you attempt that again."

The marquess cocked an eyebrow and was gone.

Samantha had recovered her composure and moved to stand before Edward. His face seemed to be made of stone. He still had not looked directly at her.

"I suppose I should thank you, Edward, for coming to my rescue, only . . . well, as that was my first kiss, perhaps it could have lasted just a *bit* longer. I shouldn't have panicked, really. I think his lordship meant well."

Edward turned, and the piercing eyes bored in on her in shocked disbelief.

"I beg your pardon. I thought I just heard you say that you welcomed subjecting your person to the mauling hands of that unprincipled viper. Surely no well-bred lady would express such a thought.''

There was cold anger in his voice, and she looked down at her feet in embarrassment.

''I suppose it is too bad of me, Edward, but he is rather . . . compelling,'' she said haltingly. ''Perhaps it was the way he kissed my wrist. And the waltz . . .''

She looked up at him then, and suddenly her eyes twinkled with mischief.

''I suppose I was overcome by his gentlemanly wiles. To be sure, if you had only instructed me on the subject earlier, I would have known how to respond.''

But if she expected to spark a smile with this sally, she had sadly misjudged the situation, for the earl's eyes instantly became slits of blue ice.

''There is no time like the present, is there, Sam?''

He reached for her hand and brought it to his lips as Samantha's eyes widened in shocked surprise. He brushed the back of her hand with a featherlight touch of his mouth and then slowly, caressing her palm with his fingers, turned her hand over to expose her slender wrist. His eyes held hers for a moment, and then gently he brought his lips down on the translucent skin. Samantha felt his warm breath on her wrist as his lips moved upward, softly tracing a circular pattern. She felt her knees grow wobbly, and Edward, seeming to sense her weakness, gently clasped her arm at the elbow. This touch generated more unaccustomed sensations, and Samantha drew a sharp intake of breath.

It was then that she became aware of the music that drifted out the open door toward them. Edward dropped his hand to her waist and slowly, almost imperceptibly, drew her into his arms and into the figures of the waltz. As they moved around the terrace, Samantha's eyes never left Edward's unreadable face. Her skin burned through the fabric where his hand rested, and her body swayed into his in a strange and unfamiliar manner that she seemed powerless to control. The cobalt eyes that held hers had none of the friendliness that she was used to seeing there. And while they did not precisely evince the predatory air that Blackwood had displayed, they nevertheless emitted a strange, disturbing sort of warmth. She was mesmerized, caught in a timeless world that suddenly had become a very strange and not unpleasant place.

The music ended at last. Abruptly Edward let her go. His voice was harsh.

"Is that sufficient, Sam, or do you require further instruction? If it is kisses you want, I suppose one man will do as well as another. I am sure that a woman who is attempting to acquire experience in these matters surely must let no opportunity pass, however unexpected."

He watched her but made no move to carry out his threat.

His sarcasm cut through the haze that had enveloped her. Samantha felt her pulse throb, but this time from a blinding anger. Edward had only intended to teach her a lesson, never mind that it made her look the fool. Suddenly he seemed a stranger, a man she did not like at all.

"I do not know what game you are about, Edward, but you have given me a thorough disgust of you! I thought you were my friend. But now I see you are so cruel and heartless that you can find no better amusement than to take advantage of a friend's ignorance. Pray give your expert lessons to someone else, and I will seek my instruction elsewhere!"

Samantha turned on her heel and marched back into the ballroom.

Left alone in the garden, Edward heard the orchestra strike up again. Another waltz. Some young buck seeking to charm his ladylove must have paid the conductor well. The lanterns twinkled about him, but Edward did not notice their glow. He found the light had vanished with Samantha's departure. His head was throbbing, his breath shallow and raw. His pulse pounded a deafening drumbeat in his ear. In the darkness, the earl of Landsdown was suddenly gifted with the sort of vision that comes in a moment of striking clarity, bringing with it a fact that, now known, gives rise to wonder that it had lain so long hidden.

He stood absolutely motionless for a long moment. Then he gave a rueful laugh and shook his head. It was some time before he returned to the house.

Chapter 6

"How about the yellow, miss? 'Twould be lovely with your hair! 'Tis such a fine day, you'll look like one of them daffodils in the park!"

Samantha merely nodded, impervious to her maid's enthusiasm and to the cheerful rays of the sun streaming in her open window this morning. Betsy was right. It was a fine day, spring at its flirtatious best. Then why was she in the doldrums?

Looking at her glass, she did not see a pretty chestnut-haired woman with troubled hazel eyes. Instead, the images of the previous night flitted before her. Lord Blackwood holding her so improperly. Lady Darrow's knowing smile. And Edward. Kissing her hand in the most disturbing fashion and drawing her into the seductive embrace of the waltz. She frowned. Her world had suddenly become something utterly foreign.

It was not merely last night and all of its new experiences that so disturbed her. Although she had tried to put it from her mind, she had felt for some time that Edward had simply not been himself. Her brow wrinkled in perplexity. Was she losing the only friend she had ever had? Samantha suddenly felt bereft.

She waved a dismissal at Betsy and walked to the
window. Below her, the courtyard had erupted in all of its
spring finery. A profusion of lilacs lined the outer beds just
beneath her window, framing a more structured arrangement of bulbs and small evergreens that edged the stone
walkways leading to a large flagstone sitting area. There
was no one there at the moment, it being still early in the
day, but in the late afternoon it was a favorite spot for Lady
Landsdown, and occasionally Edward, to take tea if the
weather were fine and there were no callers.

Edward. Samantha sighed. Their friendship was built on
unwavering honesty and mutual respect. It had never been
encumbered or strained by flirtation or the usual attractions
that made male and female relationships so silly and
tiresome. It was not, she amended, that Edward was
unattractive. Far from it. Why, she could well imagine the
startling effect of the full force of those blue eyes turned
upon a woman he admired. She felt her face color slightly
at the thought. Of course, she had never thought of him as
other than . . . Edward, and she was equally certain that
he viewed her with the same sisterly affection he reserved
for Cecelia.

She swallowed hard. There had been nothing brotherly in
his actions last night. But they were not precisely loverlike
either. If anything, there was an undercurrent of anger in his
mood. Perhaps he had simply seized on a particularly apt
manner of showing her the folly of her ways. She brightened
somewhat. Edward's anger was something she could manage, and it was much more preferable than any of the other
uncomfortable notions that hovered about the edges of her
thoughts. She squared her shoulders.

Edward sat in his study with a glum look on his face. He
was, in fact, utterly terrified that a certain chestnut-haired
young lady would walk through the door. And she would
come. He knew Samantha Compton well enough for that.
She was not one to ignore a problem when she could look
it in the eye. He only hoped this particular problem would
disappear. But he knew it would not vanish with the sort of

simple mending he performed years ago when she presented him with the shattered pieces of her favorite doll.

No, this was not a child's problem. He had virtually forced his attentions on Sam, damned near assaulted her, if truth be told. Fortunately he had stopped himself, but just on the near side of disaster. He knew he had acted and spoken shamefully. His anger—and something else—had betrayed him. Why? After all, it was not her fault that a man like Blackwood had taken advantage of her. God knows, he himself had acted little better!

What struck him to the core, however, was the thought that he might have broken the bonds between them. If he had eased her loneliness over the years, she had shown him how truly natural and loving a friendship could be in a world in which so much was false. She had trusted him, and he had taken that faith and in his anger abused it. She should not have to pay the price for the fact that he trusted no woman, not in the sense that a man must trust in order to extend the true affections of his heart. But friendship was one thing; having to confront Sam as the woman she had become was something else altogether. It left him profoundly shaken and stunned. And that was strange, for he had thought that the shell he had constructed since his affair with Catharine was incapable of providing fertile ground for the flourishing of such emotions toward the fair sex.

The door creaked. Quickly he reached for his newspaper.

"Edward?"

Her voice was wary.

Samantha looked at the newspaper as it slowly lowered to expose the shock of blond hair and then the blue eyes. His face looked so forbidding that she hesitated at the threshold. But she knew this was one conversation that must take place.

"Are you terribly angry with me still?" she asked in an unsteady voice. "For I cannot think of any other explanation for what happened last night, and so I came to beg your pardon."

She looked at him with unblinking eyes that shimmered with unshed moisture. Abruptly Edward shook his head.

"Do not be idiotic, Sam," he said nonchalantly, his eyes deliberately returning to his paper. "My fault entirely. I wanted to teach you a lesson. I keep forgetting that you do not play by the same rules as the rest of us. Shouldn't take things so to heart, or you will fail utterly at the game of flirtation. And then how will I get you off my hands?"

He turned a page and settled comfortably into his chair.

Samantha stared at him, immobilized by this speech. She was conscious of a turbulent emotion that might have been anger or something else she could not name. She fought to keep it under control, for more than anything she wanted to restore their relationship to its former easy state. She forced a smile.

"I might have known you were up to some trickery, Edward Harrowby. I suppose I have only myself to blame for venturing into waters that anyone save a green girl would know how to avoid." Her words were light, betraying none of the raging turmoil she felt.

She waited for his response, but he said nothing. Samantha studied his face and saw with a curious surprise that he was regarding her with a strange intensity. Though she could not guess at his thoughts, the sight of those piercing blue eyes almost made her falter. It was a moment before she resumed her speech, and she did so only after Edward, his features again schooled to blandness, idly began thumbing the pages of the paper.

"I know I acted the fool by allowing Lord Blackwood's attentions," she said tentatively, "but—oh, bother!"

Samantha broke off and with a wave of her hand snatched the newspaper away. "Why must you always read that blasted thing whenever I am trying to think?"

"But I did not know, my dear, that you found the task such an effort."

This, delivered in dulcet tones, prompted Samantha to burst into laughter.

"Oh, you are a complete hand, my Lord Landsdown! And you have such an easy target before you, I wonder why you do not get bored with the ease with which your arrows find their mark!"

Edward smiled, and the tension in the room lifted. Samantha sensed it, too, and turned away briefly to collect her thoughts. Hesitantly she moved closer to his chair, wondering if she dare claim a place on the stool at his feet. As if reading her thoughts, he edged the stool closer to her with the tip of his toe.

"It is just that I have been so shut away, Edward, that I find myself exceedingly drawn to the excitement of town. As for Lord Blackwood, well, I suppose he is exceptional, but I cannot help being drawn to him, too. There will be time soon enough to ponder the quiet respectability of my life after the Season is over."

She perched gingerly on the stool and looked up into his eyes. Blushing, she tried to explain further.

"You know, Edward, that truly was my first kiss," she began with uncharacteristic diffidence. "It was not at all like I had expected."

Edward arched a brow, but said only, "What, exactly, were you expecting?"

Samantha laughed shyly. "Oh, I am such a ninny! I suppose I wished for something magical, and yet something warm and welcoming that said there was a place for me . . . in someone's heart."

She shook her head at the unexpected tears that had begun to form and quickly wiped her eyes.

"I fear I am in danger of becoming a watering pot." She laughed unsteadily.

Edward silently handed her his handkerchief. Samantha blew her nose and then continued.

"Lord Blackwood's kiss was overwhelming, to be sure, and I can't say I have ever experienced such . . . sensations before," she said thoughtfully. "But there was nothing, well, nothing *friendly* about it. I know that sounds ridiculous! I can think of no other way to describe it. Perhaps it just wants time and experience." She cocked her head and smiled. "Mayhap a few more turns about the garden with Lord Blackwood . . ."

"No." Edward's voice was firm. "If my temper had not overruled my head last night, Sam, we would have had this talk then. Blackwood is evil. I know you cannot see it. No''—he broke off as she frowned—''it's not merely that you are so inexperienced, it's that your nature is too kind to immediately recognize the presence of such evil. Blackwood is a seducer, a devious conniver without reputation and acceptance in polite society. He cares only for himself, and he knows all the tricks to worm his way into a woman's heart.''

Samantha looked away from him then, her color high. The earl observed her embarrassment, and his voice softened.

''You do not need his attentions, Sam. There are many acceptable gentlemen eager to court the beautiful Miss Compton.''

At this, Samantha jerked her head around.

''If that were so, you are well to chasing them away, Edward. I declare you hovered about me like a mother hen last night. How am I to meet anyone acceptable if you act the sentry?''

Edward grimaced ruefully. ''You are right, I suppose. It is simply that I want to ensure you the proper kind of attention. Perhaps—oh hang it, Sam! Perhaps I just don't think anyone is good enough.''

A smile spread over Samantha's face. She rose and kissed Edward on the cheek.

''Goose! I should have known you had my best interests at heart. But you must let me choose for myself, Edward, don't you see?''

He looked at her and nodded.

''Yes, you are right. I will let you have your fun,'' he said quietly.

Samantha clapped her hands delightedly.

''But not with Blackwood,'' the earl added peremptorily. ''Stay clear of him, Sam. He means you no good.''

She cocked her head, and a devilish gleam came into her eye.

''Does that admonition also apply to Lady Darrow? For I do believe they are friends,'' she added with elaborate innocence.

Edward scowled. "Especially Lady Darrow. Those two play a deep game."

"But I thought she was a particular friend of yours," Samantha persisted sweetly. "At least that is what she indicated. Indeed, Edward, she spoke of you most fondly."

Edward's scowl deepened. "Lady Darrow and I were . . . friends, years ago," he said, his eyes looking straight ahead as if seeing the past.

Samantha found herself suddenly fascinated, hoping to hear more.

"But that was when I was as innocent as you and too filled with my own dreams to see that not everyone has the same intentions when it comes to . . . friendship," he said.

Samantha felt her pulse quicken, and she reached out to touch Edward's arm.

"Were you . . . in love, then?" she asked softly.

A slow, cynical smile crossed his aristocratic features, and Samantha felt a chill in her veins. There was a long silence, and then Edward shook off his faraway air. His eyes held an enigmatic look as he turned them on her.

"Not by half, my dear, not by half."

Samantha arched her brows at this quizzical response. She sensed there would be no more of this interesting tale. She was disappointed at the knowledge, but also oddly relieved. Meeting one of Edward's former lovers, for she now believed that indeed described Lady Darrow, was suddenly unsettling. It somehow again confronted her with a side of Edward that she had not previously contemplated, at least in any depth. First last night, and now this! Samantha felt a lurching in the pit of her stomach. She wanted him to remain the Edward of her childhood, and yet, that friend was inexorably disappearing in a way that she felt powerless to stop. Suddenly she felt a wave of sadness overwhelm her.

Edward studied her troubled features.

"What is it, Sam?" he asked quietly.

She looked embarrassed and then rose to leave.

"It is just that, well, things are changing, are they not?" she said in a small voice, her back to him.

Edward heard the dejection and wanted to cheer her. But he could not, for in truth she had echoed his sentiments.

"Yes, my dear, I fear they are," he said simply.

Samantha turned to look at him, her eyes pleading.

"Edward, promise we shall always stay friends," she said, and there was an urgent note in her voice. "I would never wish that to change."

He looked at her for a long moment and then forced a smile to his face.

"I promise," he said, though it sounded even to his own ears like a eulogy.

Chapter 7

Lady Darrow arranged her skirts artfully, yanked a disciplined tendril into disarray, and carefully formed her face into an enticing expression of seductive promise.

When she saw the caller her butler ushered in, however, her face fell, and her pose was abandoned for one of disappointed boredom.

"Blackwood," she acknowledged sourly.

Quentin Marvale, the marquess of Blackwood, gave a derisive laugh at her lackluster greeting.

"I should be underwhelmed at such a response, Catharine. It is fortunate, however, that the high esteem in which I hold my own person does not permit me to acknowledge any other views on the subject."

He moved to the divan on which the lady had so artfully positioned herself.

"And," he added, his face looming uncomfortably close to hers, "may I remind you, my dear, that there was a time when your reception was not so . . . restrained."

Lady Darrow, who had long since lost the ability or inclination to blush, found her face nevertheless flushed with an unaccustomed warmth. She deliberately moved away from Blackwood and fixed him with a cold stare.

"What do you want, Quentin?"

The only response was another laugh, though not one that exhibited any mirth; for Quentin Marvale was far from having any quality that might provoke genuine humor. Real laughter, in fact, would have caused his friends—had he had any to truly bear that name—to fall over in shock. The lines on his face had not been bestowed by jocularity but by dissipation and the pursuit in his thirty years of such unhealthy endeavors as might be expected to fill a lifetime. He would not, moreover, have disputed any damning appellation that a gently bred society chose to bestow on him, including those that Edward had so recently used in describing the marquess to Samantha. Lord Blackwood cared not a fig for anyone save himself.

That was what had brought him to Lady Darrow's house, an abode where he had spent quite a lot of time some years ago, but in which he had had little recent interest. Nevertheless, he fixed the lady of the house with an assessing gaze.

Lady Darrow felt a chill course through her body. Even though she could have drawn Blackwood's features in the dark, so familiar were they to her, she was always shocked anew when he turned the full force of that penetrating black stare on her.

"I am pleased that I have your attention, Catharine, for there is something you can do for me. I think it will benefit you as well—not that it matters, you understand."

He flicked a speck of lint off his black kerseymere lapel and frowned as he observed the barest smudge on his boots. His valet was neglecting his duties, it seemed. Perhaps it was time to find another. Not that he cared overmuch for such things, but it would please him to show the Compton chit that the earl of Landsdown was not the only one who could dress to the line. Although, he recalled with satisfaction, based on her response to him last night, little embellishment would be required to make Miss Samantha Compton fall squarely into his net. That thought brought him back to the present. He turned to Lady Darrow.

"As I was saying, my dear, I require you to assist me with a plan involving Miss Samantha Compton."

Lady Darrow stared at him with sudden interest.

"The chit Edward has taken under his wing, of course." Blackwood smiled. "I see I have your attention. Yes, the very same child to whom you so thoughtfully introduced me last night."

"My kind introduction, as you very well know, was done at your behest," Lady Darrow responded. "But I did not realize the girl had truly caught your interest. More's the pity for her, of course. Although, Quentin, she is certainly no child—twenty, if she's a day."

Blackwood nodded and idly stretched out his legs in a pose of careless boredom.

"Her age is of no concern to me," he replied. "No, Miss Samantha Compton is an innocent, all right, but there is about her a promising spark that I find most appealing. She will not care a fig for society's strictures—until it's too late, of course—and that is just the sort of wench I like. I have a mind to get to know her infinitely better, my dear, and you shall help me in that endeavor."

Lady Darrow gave an unladylike snort and rose from the divan.

"Your reprehensible schemes for corrupting young innocents have worked in the past, to be sure, but you seem to have forgotten that Miss Compton is under the protection of Lord Landsdown. You will never pull anything over on him, Quentin. Not now, at any event," she quickly amended.

The marquess looked at her with mock sadness.

"You don't mean to tell me, Catharine, that you would put your precious blunt on that stuffy earl? My heart is wounded to the quick," he said. "But then, of course, you have always carried a *tendre* for the worthy Edward."

For the second time that morning, Lady Darrow felt the warmth steal over her face. She looked away.

"Whatever was between Edward and me was destroyed by your interference," she said. "I do not think he will fall prey to you a second time. And if you think it, you are a fool, Quentin."

Her words sent Blackwood to his feet. He grabbed her arm and roughly forced her around. "The lady conveniently forgets her own role in that episode, I believe. For it was you, my dear, who threw young Edward over for me, if I recall events correctly." He released her arm with a suddenness that made Lady Darrow reach out for the nearest chair in order to regain her balance.

Blackwood smiled. "What a pity, my dear, that you lacked the foresight to see that Edward would come into his own wealth and title eventually. But then, women do seem to lack a certain perspective on events, do they not?"

Lady Darrow remained silent. She could not dispute Blackwood's recollection of past events, although she did not view her own behavior in such harsh terms. At the time she had betrayed Edward for the marquess's plumper purse, she had been widowed for only a year and was desperate to ensure her financial security. Lord Darrow, a man she had poorly tolerated and much disliked, had gotten his revenge for her ill-concealed scorn by leaving her with precious little but her looks.

The young Edward Harrowby had fallen in love with the beautiful widow. And she not a little with him, even though she might have given him a few years and should have been wiser. She knew her sights must remain fixed on an altogether different sort, one who could bring her quick and easy fortune. When Blackwood importuned her to cast the younger man off in favor of his own protection, she had complied, but not before Edward had discovered the two of them in a rather compromising situation. Lady Darrow still paled at the memory of the look on Edward's face. If, over the years, she had come to regret her impulsiveness, it was something she preferred to keep to herself. She suspected that time had not dulled Edward's memory of the past, judging from the air of cold implacability he adopted whenever he was in her presence. The man he had become would never again be taken in. A terrible sense of foreboding filled her as she obliquely studied Blackwood.

"My perspective is not at issue, Quentin. I believe it is yours that is at fault. Landsdown seems to be very protective of Miss Compton, and I do not believe that even a dastardly clever blackguard such as you can penetrate that fortress. Edward will never allow you to call upon her, and I cannot think you will even be allowed near her.''

Blackwood smiled and thoughtfully stroked his chin.

"It is true that Landsdown holds me in no great esteem, a condition that was perhaps exacerbated last night,'' he said. "But you move in somewhat more acceptable circles and if you were to make yourself amiable to Miss Compton, I have no doubt that I can manage the rest.''

Lady Darrow gave him an assessing gaze.

"I do not think my friendship with Miss Compton will be any more acceptable to Landsdown than yours, Quentin.''

"Ah, but there is where you are wrong, my dear. I intend that you shall make yourself quite acceptable not only to Miss Compton, but also to his lordship. You shall distract him from his vigilance over the young innocent he has under his roof.''

Lady Darrow paled.

"There is no longer anything between Edward and me, Quentin. Your plan is quite wrongheaded.''

"Ah, but you wish there to be something, do you not, Catharine? I have seen the way you look at him, and it is not simply the money, is it? The fair-haired lord has made his mark on your heart. I have discovered, in my long years of experience in such matters, that women whose affections are engaged are capable of great and surprising things.''

Blackwood smiled cynically as he watched the effect of his words upon Lady Darrow. The color had thoroughly drained from her face, and she sat down in something of a daze.

"I tell you, it would never work,'' she said at last. "He holds me in at least as much disgust as he does you.''

Blackwood reached down and caressed her face with the tip of his finger. She pulled away, and he laughed.

"But it is worth the try, my dear, is it not?'' he hissed softly into her ear. "It is ever so much worth the try.''

Lady Darrow said nothing for a long while. Her mind's eye was seeing images of a laughing young Edward presenting her with some posies at a secluded picnic. Then her thoughts strayed to the simple cottage where he had taken her after their spare al fresco meal. His deep blue eyes had grown suddenly serious, and his cleanly sculpted face had taken on a reverent air as he kissed her. The memory of the manner in which the rest of that afternoon was spent traveled like lightning across the years and sent goose bumps up her spine.

Her pulse quickened, and for the first time in a long while, Catharine Darrow felt a surge of happiness.

"Yes, Quentin, I believe it is worth the try," she said finally.

Henry Winston, Lord Formsby, nervously looked over his port at the earl of Landsdown, who seemed inexplicably morose this night. They had dined *en famille,* excepting Formsby, one of Edward's closest friends. Their association had begun at Oxford, where both had done less studying and more carousing than they should have, perhaps, but no less or more than others of their ilk.

Although both had happily left their wilder moments behind them, particularly as it concerned the indiscriminate pursuit of certain pleasures reposing in relations with the female sex, neither had found particular satisfaction in their maturity with the ladies who presented themselves for more sedate and serious unions.

In short, both Lords Formsby and Landsdown had become quite skilled at evading the marriage net. In Formsby's case, however, it was not that he had no wish to play the game. It was rather that he had not yet become acquainted with a lady who could persuade him to such exclusivity as Formsby did, in his loyal and open heart, wish to bestow upon the woman he would love. Unlike his long-disillusioned friend, Formsby did passionately hope and believe that love would come his way and that the object of his affections would not only be worthy of them, but also would return them in full measure.

Lately, however, Lord Formsby had begun to have doubts, due to the circumstance that his thoughts had been traveling in a direction that seemed to lead inexorably to Lady Cecelia Harrowby. That was worrisome. She was a diamond of the first water who could have her pick of eligible bachelors; moreover, Formsby was uncertain that Edward would view him as an eligible *parti* for his only sister. He feared that Edward, recalling some of their more lascivious pursuits, might think his friend's aims less than honorable or his suit—if it came to that—unworthy. Finally Formsby was reluctant to declare himself precipitously, since he was himself not altogether certain of his intentions. Chief among them, however, was a desire to further his acquaintance with Lady Cecelia, with whom he had heretofore had only slight social intercourse. How to do so without raising Edward's suspicions, especially if it developed that he and the lady did not suit, remained a perplexing problem.

It was one Lord Formsby was considering as he studied his friend, whose gaze seemed riveted on the patterns his port made in the swirling glass. Formsby cleared his throat.

"Hesitate to pry, Edward, but is there something amiss? Like to think your silence ain't aimed at present company."

Edward coughed abruptly and, chagrined, raised an eye to his friend.

"You are right, Henry, I've been insufferably rude. I do beg your pardon."

Edward seemed inclined to leave the matter there, but then apparently thought better of it.

"I suppose I've been trying to see into the future, an impossible task, of course." He smiled. "Merely brooding about the ladies under my roof. You don't know what it's like to have to worry about every swell who comes to call, whether his intentions are honorable, whether his income is sufficient, whether he has any mean or base instincts I can ferret out—the usual thing, you know. But I forget, you have no sisters, so you can't know. I can tell you, though, it is quite a responsibility to make certain your . . . loved ones make the right choices."

Formsby's face had grown ashen as this speech came to a conclusion, and his spirits plummeted further.

"But surely, Edward, there comes a time when the lady

must be allowed to choose for herself. And I'm sure many of the . . . gentlemen have the highest of intentions.''

Edward scoffed.

''Have your eyes been closed to the world around you, Henry? Worse, have you completely forgotten our own history? I seem to remember that neither of us had very high intentions then.''

Formsby shifted uncomfortably in his chair, but he was determined to press on.

''But surely, Edward, one's performance in youth does not condemn one forever. We have both become right responsible gentlemen, if I do say so, and had I a sister, by the bye, I would not hesitate to bestow her on you!''

This last rather odd comment, which Lord Formsby considered a masterstroke, was delivered with a triumphant flourish. Edward stared at him for a moment, and then burst into laughter.

''How generous of you, my friend, to be sure!'' he said, clapping Formsby on the back. ''I can see I would be hard-pressed to turn down such a magnanimous offer. 'Tis fortunate, is it not, that neither of us is marriage minded at the moment? I would be obliged to return the favor, and I cannot imagine you as my brother-in-law!''

With that, Edward continued to laugh as if at some private joke. While Lord Formsby was happy to see his friend in a better frame of mind, he was not thrilled at the turn the conversation had taken.

''Well, I myself might wish to marry someday . . . that is, if the right lady could be found. I am not completely beyond the pale, you know,'' Formsby said with a wounded air.

He held his breath. He had said all he was going to say about that, and he prayed he had not come too close to the bone. It would not do for Edward to think he referred especially to Lady Cecelia.

But Edward, his mood lightened considerably, appeared to have forgotten the matter. He was ready to rejoin the ladies.

"Come, Henry. Let us see what awaits in the drawing room."

Later, Lord Landsdown was to recall his friend's words with less charity, especially after he spent the rest of the evening in observation of Lord Formsby's rather concerted efforts toward Samantha.

Unnerved by their conversation, Formsby was determined to give Edward no cause to suspect his interest in Lady Cecelia, and thus gain for himself time to get to know the lady. His desperately befuddled mind searched for a way to throw Edward off his design, and at that moment his eye fell upon Miss Samantha Compton. With steely discipline he walked past the charming object of his interest and pulled a chair up close to the one in which Miss Compton was sitting with some needlework. There, in apparent rapt attention, Lord Formsby proceeded to engage her in conversation for some time. Happily he found her an amiable companion with no lack of conversation or sense, and thus the time passed quite enjoyably. Except, of course, that he was was not able to cast so much as an eye in Lady Cecelia's direction.

Edward observed the two heads close together near the fireplace and immediately experienced a return to his previous morose condition, deepened by the horrifying realization that should Henry be seriously interested in Sam, there could be no real objection to the match. Henry was as respectable and decent as any gentleman of his acquaintance, and Edward had no doubt that should Henry fix his interest in that corner, a marriage proposal would soon follow. That thought sent him well and truly into the doldrums, and the evening dragged on into oblivion.

The object of speculation was blissfully unaware that Edward already had her marching down the aisle with Lord Formsby. Samantha was, in truth, much interested in furthering her acquaintance with that gentleman, as she believed she had detected a certain interest on Lady Cecelia's part in the handsome Lord Formsby. Samantha intended to size him up for herself. In this she was happy to find much in that gentleman to please. He was well to looks, she decided,

casting him a sidelong gaze that took in his curly brown hair
and open, friendly brown eyes. He seemed kind, thoroughly
without guile and the airs she found so off-putting among
the other bachelors she had met.

Idly her thoughts wandered back to that morning, when
she and Cecelia had both found themselves up at an
unfashionably early hour and decided to take advantage of
the unusually nice weather. Accompanied by a groom, the
two ladies enjoyed a rather spirited ride in the almost
deserted park. In fact, they had not seen anyone at all until
they had turned their mounts around and headed back to
Landsdown House. Samantha's heart had risen to her throat
then, for she recognized the single rider coming toward
them. It was Lord Blackwood, whom she had not seen since
the Montrose ball several days ago.

But if Samantha thought Blackwood would again embarrass her, she was mistaken. He doffed his hat and bowed
from his position in the saddle, his conversation everything
that was respectable, although perhaps a bit florid.

"Allow me to say how charming it is to see two ladies
availing themselves of an invigorating ride this beautiful
morning. If the other flowers of the *ton* could see the lovely
glow that such pursuits bestowed upon your beautiful
cheeks, I am certain an early ride would become all the
rage."

Samantha blushed at such frankly appreciative language,
but Cecelia's eyes narrowed. For his part, Blackwood
spared only a glance for that young lady. Beautiful though
she was, as Landsdown's sister she was an inviolate target,
and too wary by far. No, the Compton chit held more
promise. There was about her a naivete that would serve
him well. Yet she was spirited, and that intrigued him even
more. He could well imagine the fireworks they would
produce.

"Allow me to escort you home," he said, fixing his
mesmerizing eyes on Samantha, "for I gather you are
headed in that direction."

"As we are properly attended, our direction should give
you no concern, my lord. And I am sure we would not wish

to keep you from your business," Lady Cecelia said with mock sweetness.

What might have been a scowl creeping across Blackwood's features became a smile at Samantha's next words.

"I am sure we should be grateful for Lord Blackwood's kind escort, Cecelia," Samantha heard herself saying. "Though to be sure," she amended, "we would not wish to keep you from anything pressing."

"There is nothing more pressing than making certain that two such beautiful ladies arrive safely home at their door," Blackwood said gallantly and, deftly maneuvering his horse next to hers, set a sedate pace that would not bring them to Landsdown House in any great haste.

Cecelia said nothing during the return trip, but Samantha found herself drawn into conversation with the man with a mixture of interest and apprehension. Although his demeanor was unexceptional, there was about him an air of barely restrained power. It was as if at any moment she might find herself in the grip of those huge hands and under the spell of those black eyes. It was a prospect that was not a little tantalizing, at least from the safe perspective of horseback in a public park not a great distance from her door.

When they were inside, Cecelia rang her a peal.

"How could you encourage that odious man, Samantha? Edward would be outraged!"

Samantha colored guiltily, remembering the scene in the Montrose garden.

"I expect you are right, Cecelia, but you must admit he was all that was correct, and I rather think Lord Blackwood's reputation is exaggerated, in any case," she replied.

The recollection of Blackwood's bruising kiss in the garden, however, caused her to add: "Or at least, perhaps he is trying to make amends for his behavior."

That comment produced a biting laugh from her companion.

"Oh, really, Samantha! Do not prove Edward insufferably right by demonstrating so effectively that you do not know what the game is about! I trust you have better sense than to believe that a leopard can change its spots!'' With that she lifted the hem of her skirt and began to ascend the stairs. "Do not think I will go running to Edward with this tale, Samantha, but do have a care, for I do not trust that man at all!''

Samantha pondered those words as she listened with half an ear to Lord Formsby. Lord Blackwood was undoubtedly unconventional and probably not little a dangerous. Still, he was the perfect model for "Lord Devil." And he could certainly enliven an evening! She giggled, causing Lord Formsby to break off mid sentence and provoking a deepening scowl from the opposite corner of the room, where Edward sat pondering the future.

Chapter 8

The ball for Lady Cecelia Harrowby and Miss Samantha Compton was to be one of the Season's more noteworthy events, as the Landsdown consequence, not to mention wealth, was of the highest order. And although it was by now well known that Miss Compton had not a feather to fly with, it was reliably rumored that Landsdown himself was prepared to settle a not insignificant sum upon her. While Miss Compton's looks did not tend toward the unrivaled beauty of the Incomparable Lady Cecelia, they were nevertheless judged to be uncommonly fine. Moreover, her fresh conversation and unusual spirit had caused her to be considered something of an Original. Thus, Miss Compton's prospects, while not discussed in the same breath as those of Lady Cecelia, were widely viewed as quite acceptable.

And so it was with great anticipation that Lady Landsdown went about planning the event. That feeling was shared by Lady Cecelia, who, as expected, had been deluged with suitors and could be counted upon to be the brightest star in the evening's firmament. The earl, meanwhile, studiously avoided all attempts to draw him into the planning, merely saying he could contribute little that his inestimable mother had not already considered.

Samantha also looked forward to the ball, although her feelings were mixed. For one thing, Lord Blackwood was not to be invited, having been deemed ineligible for such a refined gathering in honor of two reigning innocents. It was not that Samantha had formed a *tendre* for him, precisely, for she acknowledged his thorough unsuitability as a match for any virtuous young lady. That, however, did not prevent her from being fascinated by his reputation, mesmerized by his physical attributes, and not a little eager to observe such a creature in action. There was, she could not deny, a certain fearsome thrill she felt in his presence, a happenstance that had occurred more often in recent days, which was rather odd, considering that Edward had forbidden any such encounters.

There was, for instance, the occasion at the opera, when Lord Blackwood had greeted her outside their box during intermission after Edward had unaccountably been called away. Lady Cecelia had frowned dismissively in Blackwood's direction, but he had ignored that unmistakable signal and bowed over Samantha's hand, placing upon it a tantalizingly brief kiss.

Once, leaving an afternoon performance at Astley's, the Landsdown group had come upon Lady Darrow in great distress at the breakdown of her carriage. It had been necessary for Edward to see to the matter, and so he had temporarily left their group, which included Samantha, Cecelia, and Lady Alynn. Blackwood suddenly appeared and gallantly offered to escort the ladies home. While Cecelia and Alynn were discussing this proposition, the marquess maneuvered Samantha to the side and engaged her in conversation.

"Alas, my fair charmer, I have been in an agony of anticipation of seeing your lovely face. Do you, by any chance, go to the Melwoods' ball on the morrow? For I could endure the waiting if only I could be assured of a dance one day hence."

Samantha greeted this fulsome declaration with a laugh.

"Lord Blackwood, I fear you are coming it too brown! Your words do an injustice, for only a paragon could be worthy of such inspiration. I am only a country miss, as you know, and inspire raptures only from the dressmaker, who sees the enormous sums spent to drape this inelegant figure in the fabrics of fantasy.''

Blackwood raised his brow at this frank response and gave her a disarming smile. Then he bent toward her face with a look that thoroughly erased Samantha's disparaging grin.

''How delightfully improper of you to have raised the topic, my dear, but since you have, I can assure you that one would have to be blind to think your figure . . . inelegant. From my observation—''

''Lord Blackwood!'' Samantha interrupted, her face flushing to the roots of her hair. ''I am sure it is most ungentlemanly of you to turn my unfortunate words to such ill use!''

Blackwood accepted the rebuff, observing her embarrassment with silent satisfaction.

''Then let us dwell on it no more, Miss Compton. Consider your words forgiven, if not forgotten. You cannot ask a man such as I to ignore completely the charms that radiate from your lovely person.''

As a mortified Samantha seemed about to turn on her heel at this comment, Blackwood hastily continued, ''But you distract me from my purpose, which is to ascertain if indeed you are promised to the Melwoods'. For I could not call the evening happy if I could not stand up with you for at least one dance.''

He punctuated this request with an innocent, pleading smile that had Samantha wondering if she had been in error in taking offense at his earlier remarks. Perhaps she was too hasty to believe the worst of him, she reasoned. And so she was somewhat mollified when she replied.

''I do believe we are to attend the Melwoods', though I cannot promise to save you a dance,'' she said frankly.

Disappointment and what might have been anger flitted across his face.

She hesitated for a moment and added resolutely: ''Lord Blackwood, you must know that Lord Landsdown does not precisely approve of our acquaintance. Edward is my friend as well as the head of the household in which I am residing. I cannot contravene his wishes, though I might add, sir, that I have thought it a pity society judges you so harshly. I cannot precisely approve of your demeanor, but I do not believe that you mean ill. Perhaps you have merely been out of proper circles for so long that you have forgotten how to go on. I share the same feeling myself upon occasion, having had little experience heretofore with London ways.''

Lord Blackwood listened to this speech in utter amazement. Miss Compton was an Original, that much was certain. They would rub along quite nicely, he thought, his interest intensified. He bowed gravely.

''I hope I am not being presumptuous in offering thanks that I appear to have at least one noble defender, Miss Compton. Would that the rest of society shared your generous fair-mindedness. I earnestly hope I can live up to your opinion of me.'' He gingerly took her hand, kissed it lingeringly, and walked away, leaving a flustered Samantha watching his progress.

That encounter had not gone unnoticed by Lady Cecelia. It was clear from her face that she was resolved to speak to Edward about these occasional meetings, about which Cecelia had her suspicions. But in this Samantha was favored by the arrival of Lord Formsby, whose presence quite drove that notion from Lady Cecelia's head, at least for the moment. So it was that Edward returned from his gallant but reluctant efforts on Lady Darrow's behalf to behold Lord Formsby surrounded by three ladies whose glowing cheeks were not entirely caused by the brisk breeze that had whipped up that afternoon. Edward contemplated the unnatural color that seemed particularly evident on Samantha's face and silently cursed Lord Formsby, Catharine Darrow, and his own stupidity.

They had not, after all, managed the Melwoods' ball, Lady Landsdown having come down with the headache. Edward had taken himself to his club, having declared himself unwilling to shoulder alone the responsibility for chaperoning two such popular young debutantes. Samantha was surprised to find herself only slightly disappointed and happily spent the evening entertaining Cecelia with selections from Mrs. Edgeworth's latest book.

In the ensuing days, Samantha spent much spare time writing busily, often in her room, sometimes in the library when it was unoccupied. "Lord Devil" had completely taken over her story, she found, and she had to force herself to give her heroine, Juliana Morriston, equal attention. Lord Blackwood's character greatly improved as she translated and embellished his qualities in the dramatic Lord Deverill. "Lord Devil," she decided, was thoroughly misunderstood and condemned by society, simply because he had been disappointed in love and taken to live in a drafty old castle, rumored to be haunted, along the Thames. Only Juliana seemed to possess the strength of character and resolve to brave the fortress of his defenses, and Samantha found her own pulse quickening when she cast the helpless Juliana literally at Lord Devil's door, the result of an unfortunate carriage accident that rendered her only attendant, a maid, unconscious, along with their coachman.

> *Juliana eyed the forbidding servant who had come to the door to listen impassively as she described her plight.*
>
> *"Lord Deverill does not see visitors," the dour footman pronounced rigidly, and it seemed as if his eyes grew large and menacing as he studied her bedraggled appearance.*
>
> *With tears in her eyes, Juliana stood helplessly at the door, desperately searching her brain for a course of action that might save the lives of her maid and coachman. Suddenly the deafening silence was rent by a low, velvet-smooth voice.*
>
> *"Miss Morriston."*
>
> *She jumped and felt, rather than saw, Lord Deverill at her side. Her elbow burned where his hand moved to support it, and she thought she would lose her breath in the maelstrom of swirling emotions that had erupted*

*in the darkened castle, filling her gentle mind with
terror and fear.*

*I am lost, she thought, trembling as the black eyes
captured hers.*

*"I have been in an agony of anticipation of seeing
your lovely face," the voice said, and the deep tones
echoed off the rough-hewn rock of the darkened foyer.
"That you have arrived at my door can only mean that
I am fortunate to have at least one noble defender. I
earnestly hope I can live up to your opinion of me."*

*As Juliana heard the words, they seemed to take on
a physical presence, transfigured into a thick, gray fog
that enveloped her body, lifting it up into a pair of
strong arms. She realized, too late, that she was about
to faint.*

Samantha sat back in the overstuffed library chair that
was Edward's favorite and frowned. She was not quite
certain what Juliana had meant by "I am lost." It seemed
ominous enough, but somehow imprecise. She put down her
pen, uncertain what would happen next to Juliana and Lord
Deverill. She needed some inspiration, she decided. Perhaps
tomorrow night's ball would provide it, although it was a
pity that Lord Blackwood was not invited. She thoroughly
understood the Landsdowns' sentiments on that score, but
she could not suppress a wistful recollection of the waltz
they had shared at the Montrose ball. There was something
charged about his presence, even though it was rather
disturbing. With that thought in her brain and a lazy smile
on her face, Samantha closed eyes and drifted off.

In her dream, the music floated to the terrace where
Samantha and Lord Blackwood were dancing, and she
smiled at the piercing eyes that looked down at her with an
adoring expression. He was speaking, and she somehow
could not make out the words. But they seemed to reassure
her of his intention to conduct himself as a gentleman
worthy of a gently bred young lady such as herself. She
smiled back as the terrace suddenly became very hazy and
Lord Blackwood enveloped her in a constricting embrace.

His face bent closer and suddenly became a distorted mask of anger and evil. The eyes looked daggers at her own shocked countenance, and his mouth had become a leering specter of disdain. A gray, ghostlike castle suddenly loomed behind him, its door a great gaping hole that promised only terror within. She knew a moment of panic and lashed out at the arms that had tightened around her.

"No!" she cried. "I'll not dance with the devil! Let me go!" Samantha began struggling for all she was worth.

Her thrashing arm barely missed the finely chiseled nose of Lord Landsdown, who was endeavoring to waken Samantha from what looked like a most unpleasant dream. He shook her shoulders again and was at last rewarded when her eyelashes opened to reveal a pair of hazel eyes that bore a singular look of confused terror. She blinked for a moment and stared in perplexity at his face, no more than a few inches from her own. At last she relaxed her features.

"Oh, Edward!" she said with a dismayed sigh. "I see I have disgraced myself with a case of the hysterics. But it is comforting to see that it is you and not . . . anyone else."

The earl's brows rose at that remark as he surveyed the clearly shaken young lady before him.

"And just whom did you fear to see, Sam?" he asked quietly.

She colored.

"No one, really. I'm afraid I have let my fantasies get away with me. One of my characters fully took hold of my brain for a moment, that's all."

His eyes strayed to the manuscript pages that had fallen from her hand to the floor.

"Lord Devil, perhaps?"

He found the answer in her silence and bent to scoop up the pages.

"Sam, is it really sensible to devote so much time to this . . . nonsense? I cannot think that it is altogether healthy for an impressionable young lady to spend so much time spinning fantasies. Furthermore . . ."

Her indignant look stopped him mid sentence, and he sighed in resignation.

"Spare me your outraged defenses, Sam. I did not mean to disparage your work," he said, smiling. "It is only that I imagine there are many more interesting things of the present with which to occupy one's time. Most young ladies, for instance, would be eagerly anticipating their ball, yet you prefer to while away the time in the library dreaming about menacing fribbles. I'm afraid I do not understand it."

"Oh, but I am exceedingly gratified about the ball," Samantha said quickly, thinking guiltily about the small fortune that Edward was spending on the event. "I might not be quite the smashing success as Cecelia, to be sure," she added, "but I will endeavor to live up to all of Lady Landsdown's expectations."

"Fustian!" Edward exclaimed. "Such self-effacement does not become you, Sam. I have seen the court that surrounds you. Indeed, it has caused me no small anxiety to investigate each and every one of your gallants to ascertain their appropriateness and suitability."

He paused a moment, rolling a thought over in his head. Then he fixed her with a stern gaze.

"Do not think to gammon me with false modesty, Sam. I shall not be lulled into relaxing my vigilance, although I should simply wash my hands of you. Any man who wins you will undoubtedly deserve the merry chase you will lead him!"

He rocked back on his heels and surveyed her face, which was in a fair way to being overtaken by a smile she was trying hard to suppress. Finally she gave up the effort and laughed outright.

"You wrong me, Edward, but I blush at your judgment. Can you really think that all of the pinks who pay me court are seriously considering offering for my hand? You refine too much on the flirtatious proclivities of your set, I'm afraid. I am certain that they are only satisfying their curiosity about the eccentric Miss Compton. Or perhaps they are merely trying for the outer reaches of Cecelia's orbit."

"So you have become an expert, have you, on flirtation?'' he countered in a quiet voice. ''Pray where did you acquire that knowledge? For I seem to remember a request not too long ago for instruction on that very score. Have you succeeded, then, in finding someone to accommodate you?''

Samantha blushed but refused to avert her eyes from Edward's unaccountably stern face. Finally she rose and briskly arranged her skirts.

''If it were anyone but you reading me such a lecture, Edward, I would swear 'twas jealousy! But as I know you are so far from having any such notions in your head—indeed, any quantity of warm regard or sensibility for one of my sex—I can only conclude that my judgment is as flawed as yours.''

With that, Samantha swept from the library, leaving Edward glaring in her wake.

The Landsdown ball was a truly magnificent occasion. Carriages clogged Charles Street and Berkeley Square back to Grosvenor and down to Piccadilly as the *ton* waited to enter the stately house, the staff of which had outdone itself this evening.

The oak and brass had been polished to a warm glow that reflected years of care by the servants of generations of Landsdowns. Many of those ancestral worthies peered out from the gilded frames that adorned the ballroom, and Samantha wondered if they looked upon the gathering with not a little envy at the magnificence and splendor displayed before their eyes.

She was astonished and gratified by her own appearance, which had been orchestrated by her maid Betsy with the same care that would have attended preparations for a court presentation. Her gown of sea-green sarcenet was trimmed with golden ribbon that echoed the golden glow from the topaz ear bobs and the simple pendant she had worn at the Montrose gala. The gown exposed her bare shoulders, which seemed to take on a honeyed blush in the candlelight. Tiny sea-green beads edged the gold ribbon, which trimmed the neckline and fell from a delicate band just under her

bosom. Betsy had caught her heavy chestnut hair with a
gold band, from which thin tendrils escaped to frame her
face. A single topaz had been placed amid the thick tresses,
and it twinkled under the lights like a shimmering star.

Samantha quite dazzled the sea of gentlemen who vied
for a dance, and soon her card was quite full. Edward, who
had presented Cecelia and Samantha each with tiny peach
blossom corsages, danced the first set with Cecelia, as did
Lord Formsby with Samantha. For the second set, they
exchanged partners.

Heady with the excitement of the evening, Samantha
stared up into Edward's closed face and thought, not for the
first time, what a pity it was that they seemed so often these
days at daggers drawn. She knew he had only her best
interests at heart, but it irritated her that he was so set on
playing the role of stuffy guardian. His eyes, she noticed,
were on this occasion fixed at a point somewhere past her
shoulder, his expression totally blank.

"Edward, must you present the room a gift of your
complete boredom at the chore of partnering me?" she
asked, her nose wrinkled in irritation, as they came together
in the figures of the dance. "It is just a country dance, after
all, and will be over before long. Perhaps for a few moments
we could at least seem to be in charity."

Startled, the earl missed a step and ungallantly trod on her
foot.

"I beg your pardon, Sam. I suppose I have been woolgathering," he said, bringing his eyes to her face with effort.

"Well, that is most flattering, of course. Lord Landsdown
can always be counted on to give a lady a proper understanding of her worth, and just when my head is in danger
of being turned by the very flower of the *ton*'s bachelors."

The hazel eyes twinkled up at him mischievously and
brought a sheepish smile to his face.

"My inattentiveness is unforgivable, my dear, but it
should count as no reflection on you. I have indeed noticed
the gentlemen buzzing around you, like bees to honey, I
might add, all angling for a turn about the ballroom with the
very interesting Miss Compton," he said lightly.

Samantha tapped his arm playfully with the fan that dangled at her wrist. They separated again, and this time Edward's eyes did not leave her.

When the dance brought them together again, Edward whispered into her ear. "I should ask, I expect, whether any particular gentleman has been fortunate enough to find especial favor. By rights, I should be the first to know."

"Don't be impertinent, Edward," Samantha retorted. "You must bide your time like all the rest. Although in truth I cannot say that anyone has absolute claim to my affections."

Edward frowned.

"Absolute?" he repeated, perplexed.

But his question was lost as the orchestra launched into a particularly lively movement that prevented further speech. When the dance ended, he relinquished Samantha to one of the more adoring members of her court, a Mr. Daniel Worthington. That gentleman was hardly dry behind the ears, in Edward's judgment, and always managed to stare at Samantha with large pleading calf eyes that made Edward want to laugh out loud. The earl had nevertheless learned that the calfling was entirely eligible by virtue of his connections with Lord Wexford and a sizable income of ten thousand pounds a year. Still, Edward had only contempt for the lad, who would never have the gumption to handle Sam.

The earl stared glumly after the couple as they whirled away. Samantha, far from looking uninterested in Worthington, was smiling brilliantly up at him. For his part, Mr. Worthington seemed catapulted into raptures by the mere presence of his goddess. And she was a goddess tonight, Edward acknowledged. That dress swirled gracefully and tantalizingly around her figure, and the color brought out her eyes and that rich, chestnut hair. He could hardly recall the awkward young girl of his youth. There was nothing gawky about her now. Despite her stated fears, it was clear she would have no trouble finding a husband this Season. There were probably a dozen gentlemen half in love with her already, he surmised. None of them worthy, he thought sourly, but all of them highly eligible.

Edward turned away from the scene in the ballroom and stepped out onto the courtyard. He knew he should be pleased at Sam's conquests, but the fact remained that he was not. He should be delighted that so many eligible gentlemen were eager to take her off his hands, but he was not. He should be happy that Sam would find a husband to provide for her and her mother and thrilled that her future was probably only days away from being settled.

But he was not. And he knew the reason why, indeed, had known it for some time. To his great and everlasting dismay, the earl of Landsdown knew himself in a state far removed from the companionable affection in which he had held Samantha Compton for all the years of their youth. No, it was much more than that, and he was utterly appalled at it. Sam, he knew, regarded him with an abiding respect and affection that bespoke deep friendship—but nothing more. Sam would be mortified if she knew his true feelings. Worse, he would surely lose the friendship he cherished.

Edward frowned. He had intended to help her find a husband, an intention formed before the blinders had fallen from his eyes, although he had always viewed the prospect with some reluctance. But the disturbing observation that not a few dazzled swains seemed likely to come up to scratch now left him unable to avoid confronting his feelings. He knew Sam would do her duty to provide for her mother. She would choose one of them.

Why could she not choose him? It was utterly unthinkable, of course, but so was his current state. And although a declaration from him now was out of the question—it would shock her senseless, no doubt—perhaps over time her thoughts could be led in that direction. Edward smiled thoughtfully. The Season was still young. Sam would make no hasty decisions, and so he could afford to bide his time. Ever so slowly, he would win her. It would have to be done carefully—she was under his very roof, after all, and that could work to his advantage as well as frighten her off. But if it were done properly, she would never suspect his game.

Edward smiled more broadly as his confidence grew. It was not an easy challenge, but he would win, of course. Women had always found him irresistible. He fancied that he was not arrogant or overimpressed with this fortuitous quality; still, it would serve him in good stead. He rubbed his hands together against the slight chill and turned back toward the dancers and the twinkling candlelight. With a little friendly persuasion, Samantha Compton would be his before summer.

Samantha stared up at Lord Formsby. Their dance was a waltz, and she found it rather pleasant to be in his arms, even though she had no thoughts of him other than as a candidate for Cecelia's hand. To her way of thinking, he was out of the ordinary way of those too-flattering dandies who fawned over Cecelia and worshipped her every word. He seemed more serious, somehow, and more genuine, though he kept his thoughts to himself. She thought he seemed intent on playing his own game, though it was unclear just what that was.

He was a very handsome man, she acknowledged, with warm brown eyes and a dimple that punctuated one side of his face when he was amused. She sighed. That her heart was unmoved by such a gentleman was really too bad. But in truth she had been singularly untouched by any she met. There was only one who had made her pulse race, and that did not bear thinking of. Well, she amended, there was Edward, that night at the Montroses'. But he was just punishing her for flouting his wishes. Edward was the last man who would think of her in *that* way. Not only did he look upon most of her sex with contempt, but also he thought of her only as a friend he was obligated to help marry off.

Still, when she looked up at Lord Formsby's brown eyes, she somehow wished that they were cobalt blue. She could not stifle one tiny shred of curiosity about how Edward would act with a woman he really and truly loved. Shocked at the direction her thoughts were taking, she pasted a congenial smile on her face and laughed too loudly at a comment Lord Formsby was making.

That gentleman wrinkled his forehead in perplexity.

"Miss Compton, is there anything amiss?" he asked solicitously.

"Why, Lord Formsby, whyever should you think it?" was her gay reply.

"No reason. Beg your pardon. It is merely that you seem to be . . . not yourself, precisely. Forgive me, I do not wish to offend." He looked down at her with concern.

"As if you could offend me, my lord, for I well know that you are the most amiable and well-intentioned of gentlemen," she said, and was gratified to see his brow smooth. "But if I may speak frankly, sir, may I say that I am surprised you are not dancing this waltz with Cecelia. I can assure you she is much more graceful at the dance than I."

Formsby colored, and Samantha knew a moment of guilt at her boldness. But her words were quite deliberate, for she had intended to gauge his reaction. She had noticed that Cecelia often watched Lord Formsby intently when she thought herself unobserved. Samantha had detected similar glances from Lord Formsby. While his lordship had been cordial to Cecelia, however, he had not shown her any distinctive partiality. Samantha could not imagine the reason for this, unless perhaps he was not certain of his feelings or was loath to face the stiff competition. But Samantha suspected that Lord Formsby was made of sterner stuff. She was pleased to see the flush steal across his face, a possible indication that there was more in his heart than he had revealed.

"As to that, Miss Compton, you are every bit as graceful a dancer as Lady Cecelia. Her card is full, at all events. Has all the partners she can manage," he replied, and then added hastily, "as you do, to be sure."

"Nonsense, Lord Formsby!" Samantha replied. "My dance card is also full, of course, but as I am one of the honorees at this ball, that is not to be remarked upon. Moreover, I hope you do not think that whom a lady chooses to dance with is any indication of her preferences.

I am persuaded that Lady Cecelia would be delighted to grant you a second dance were one of her promised partners to find himself suddenly engaged otherwise.''

A mischievous look flitted across Samantha's face.

''I do believe, my lord, that another waltz is planned after the country dance. I am promised to Edward, but that does not signify. I shall discover who is promised to Cecelia. Perhaps that gentleman will find himself distracted, leaving her dreadfully abandoned, unless someone is kind enough to rescue her.''

She looked innocently into Lord Formsby's face, over which an assortment of expressions, ranging from shock to delight, was racing.

Finally an amused smile crossed his face.

''Miss Compton, you are a most unusual young lady,'' he said. ''Never before had a proper appreciation of your abilities.''

Edward entered the ballroom to see Samantha and Henry looking at each other with such silly grins that it took him aback. Well, if Henry thought to outmaneuver the earl of Landsdown, he was seriously mistaken. With a determined air, Edward began making his way across the room. Samantha was to dance the next waltz with him, and it was the perfect time to engage his plan. He smiled.

But when Edward came to claim his dance, he found to his dismay that Samantha intended to beg off.

''I cannot, Edward, for I am utterly fatigued and about to die of thirst. I don't suppose you would care to fetch me a glass of negus?'' She smiled sweetly up at him, and he could not suppress a surge of irritation.

''I am certain any of your swains would gladly have performed such a service. I suppose I am to be honored that you have chosen to bestow upon me the role of errand boy?'' he said brusquely.

''Why, how ungallant of you, Edward! I can see you are miffed at losing your dance. I thought you, of all people, would understand. It is not as though you will die of a broken heart, you know,'' she replied gaily. ''I shudder to think of the consequences of denying a waltz to, say, Mr.

Worthington. Why, I would fear for his health! Don't be such a bear, Edward!"

With that the earl scowled and set off for the punch bowl. The moment he had gone, Samantha darted over to Cecelia, who was about to take the hand of Lord Throckmorton. Samantha frowned. She had hoped to head Throckmorton off before he reached Cecelia. Now, desperate measures were called for. She reached out and firmly clasped his lordship's arm.

"My lord, please help me! I fear I can scarcely breathe! Will you escort me to the terrace? I think I may faint!"

Lady Cecelia's eyes grew round and then narrowed in irritation. Samantha Compton had never swooned in her life. It was too bad of her to attempt such a blatant theft of her dance partner!

Lord Throckmorton looked at the young lady who was grasping his arm and then cast a wistful eye in Lady Cecelia's direction. But he knew his duty toward a lady in distress, and he wore his most practiced expression of concern as he led Samantha toward the windows. Lady Cecelia, left standing alone, glared in their direction; but a discreet cough and a male voice over her shoulder nearly made her jump.

"Beg your pardon, Lady Cecelia. Might I hope to find you without a partner at the moment? Pleasure to claim this dance in his stead."

Lady Cecelia flushed as she recognized the voice. She turned and beheld Lord Formsby's steady brown eyes, which held hers in a most determined manner. She offered her hand and moved unhesitatingly toward him.

"I was indeed bereft, my lord," she said, her lashes fluttering as her extraordinary azure eyes met his steady gaze. "But I see that situation has been remedied."

Edward looked glumly at the sight of Samantha and Lord Throckmorton vanishing through the doors to the garden and knew with certainty that if she had ever been thirsty, she had long since forgotten it. He would go after them, of course, both to maintain the proprieties and to show that mischievous imp that he was on to her game, which apparently involved blatant flirtation with every eligible male in the room. That species obviously did not include him.

His spirits had plummeted. Samantha Compton presented much more of a challenge than his scheming had anticipated. He must, he decided, be completely mad.

Chapter 9

The wind felt delightful. It was refreshing not to have a care about its effect on her hair or on the silly plumed riding hat that she had purposefully left behind this morning. Why it was necessary to deck oneself out like a fashion plate simply to ride one's horse would forever elude her, Samantha supposed. She noted happily that the park was nearly deserted. It was not fashionable to show oneself too early in the day, yet another aspect of town life that occasionally made her yearn for the simplicity of the country.

They were riding at a brisk pace. Although Edward would not countenance a full-fledged gallop, Samantha noticed that he did not cavil at the fast trot she had set. In fact, he seemed more than eager to match her neck for neck, and she was quite pleased that the little mare he had provided for her use was up to the challenge. The horse had not the pluck of Captain, of course, but then many of the spirited pleasures embedded in country life seemed to find only pale imitations in town.

Samantha stifled a sigh. It was not that she was becoming bored with her Season. But the endless parties, beautiful ballgowns, and attentive gentlemen were beginning to fill her with a sense of dissatisfaction. The social whirl had been exciting, especially at first, but as the weeks passed, she began to feel impatient with pleasures that, for lack of any better description, seemed increasingly superficial and mired in unrelenting sameness. One party was really no different from the next, and one dance partner barely distinguishable from his predecessor. Samantha mentally gave herself a shake. She was not a child anymore, and she could ill afford to indulge in this kind of reflection. Her goal, after all, was to find a husband. It was not necessary to enjoy the process.

She glanced over at Edward. She had been surprised when he offered to accompany her this morning, especially as he had been cold and aloof since their ball last week. But this morning he had been very agreeable, almost like the Edward of old. They had dismissed her groom, as that formality had never been observed between them, and Samantha had thrown herself into the ride with abandon. With the despised hat left behind on a hall table, Samantha's hair had long since been swept into disarray and was even now blowing about her face in a most undignified fashion. Her cheeks were pink with the morning's exertion, and her eyes sparkled as she set her mount to the task of beating Edward's to the persimmon tree at the spot where the path veered into a grove of trees.

When Edward saw what she was about, he instantly spurred his horse to meet her challenge. All pretense of holding the animals back was abandoned for an all-out race to the finish. Samantha saw Edward's roan shoot by, reaching the tree a second before she did. But far from begrudging Edward's victory, she burst into laughter at the result of his exertions.

"Why, Edward! So the most proper Landsdown does have a gallop or two in him! Although I do believe your cravat is a bit askew. I am sure you would not wish to be discovered at such a disadvantage! Shall we dismount so you may repair your disrepair?" she trilled, casting a pointed gaze at the unprepossessing state of Edward's normally magnificent neckwear, now wilted beyond redemption.

Edward merely raised an eyebrow, and Samantha took

that as leave to continue her speech, which had become somewhat giddy with the exhilaration of their exertion.

"Only think if someone should ride by and see the fastidious earl of Landsdown in such a state! The social disaster such a discovery must bring is to be avoided at all cost, I am sure you will readily agree!"

By now there was no disguising the amused gleam in his eye.

"We will indeed pause here, my dear, so that you may catch your breath from your wordy and altogether ill-advised pronouncements," he said and dismounted, reaching up to help her down.

Samantha was puzzled to find her pulse unsteady as his hands caught her about the waist and set her firmly on the ground. That he did not remove them immediately added to her consternation, and as she looked up into his face, she found the cobalt eyes regarding hers with a boyish twinkle. His tousled hair gave him the look of one who had only just risen, she noticed, and was shocked at the inappropriateness of such a thought.

"I can see by your remarks that you are merely attempting to gloss over your own defeat in this highly unseemly race, Sam," he said with his best mock hauteur although Samantha registered not his tone, but his nearness and the hands at her waist.

"Nevertheless," he continued, seemingly unaware of her discomfiture, "I take leave to point out that your own demeanor leaves something to be desired. Only put your mind to the scandal that might be raised if one of the Season's most pursued young ladies were discovered galloping about the park with an eligible gentleman, unaccompanied by a groom, and with little or no attention given to such proprieties as dress!"

That startling remark was punctuated by a sharp elevation of the earl's eyebrows and a slight smile that evidently was meant to cast the matter as a joke. Samantha tossed back her hair nervously. Edward's hands fell away from her waist and she found herself breathing somewhat easier.

"Must you always give one lessons in deportment,

Edward?'' she asked in irritation. ''Furthermore, I hope I
may not be said to be improperly dressed. All I have done
is to leave off that stuffy hat! And well I might wish to send
this cursed sidesaddle to join it! You and your *tonnish*
friends seem most determined to take all the joy out of
riding! Moreover, the absence of a groom is unremarkable,
I am sure, since you and I never stand on such ceremony.''

''Nevertheless,'' Edward said sternly, as he placed her
hand on his arm and led them to a small, secluded bench,
''you would do well to pin up your hair again to avoid
inviting speculation that can only be as unwanted as it is
unfounded.''

Samantha turned to him with wide eyes.

''Well, of course it is unfounded!'' she said, amazed.
''How could anyone think otherwise? Why, we are but
friends and you are . . . merely Edward!''

What might have been a pained expression flitted across
the earl's face, but it was quickly replaced by a smile.
Observing Samantha's distress, Edward patted her arm
reassuringly.

''There, there. I am certain that no one would contemplate anything out of the ordinary between us, my dear,'' he
said comfortingly. ''Indeed, I am sure we could spend
eternity in each other's presence without the slightest
improper thought occurring to either of us.''

As he spoke, his hand drifted down her arm and clasped
her hand, his thumb absentmindedly stroking her palm as
his gaze wandered to a squirrel digging at the base of an oak
tree. His other hand reached over to lightly touch her arm,
his fingers trailing idly up and down her skin.

Samantha fought an impulse to reclaim her hand and run
back to her mare. Not that Edward had the least sensibility
of what he was doing, but there was something highly
unsettling about his constant stroking. Her hand began to
feel warm and moist, and there was no reason for that on
such a brisk day. Inadvertently, she shivered. The movement instantly drew Edward's attention.

''Are you cold?'' he asked with obvious concern as he
released her hand and moved his arm to rest lightly around

her shoulders. Bending his face close to hers, he watched her with gentle and entirely brotherly regard.

Samantha wanted to scream. His arm on her shoulders generated a strange warmth that slowly was beginning to envelop her whole being. And it was having the unsettling effect of making her heart pound so loudly against her chest that it must surely be audible. What in the world was wrong with her? She was sitting on a park bench with Edward, of all people, in the most ordinary of circumstances. So why were her senses erupting in such a confusing manner? This would not do at all!

"Perhaps it is a bit chilly," she ventured hesitantly. "I suppose we should be getting back."

Edward was on his feet instantly and reached down to pull her up. His hands rested on her shoulders as Samantha stood a bit unsteadily, feeling oddly shy in his presence.

"By all means, let us return," he said. "I would not wish to risk your health. Although I disremember when Miss Samantha Compton has given evidence of a frail constitution. Do you think, my dear, that you are quite the thing?"

Samantha blushed as she looked into his eyes. There was nothing there but concern, she saw, and did not know if the knowledge brought her relief or disappointment.

"Perhaps not," she said slowly. "Mayhap I will ask my maid for a posset later. Yes, that might be just the thing."

She took the arm he offered, her thoughts a jumble. When they reached the horses, it seemed most natural for him to lift her onto her mount, but it nearly made her jump out of her skin. His brow furrowed as he observed her reaction.

"I believe we would do well to get you back posthaste," he said, patting her hands reassuringly.

"Yes, Edward, I believe we would," was her quiet reply, as they turned their horses in the direction of Landsdown House.

It was not until much later, in the solitude of her room that night, that Samantha allowed herself to reflect on the morning's events. It could not be said to be an altogether voluntary reflection, for it was undertaken chiefly in the absence of any ability or inclination to sleep. Indeed, every time Samantha closed her eyes, her mind offered her an image of Edward's strong, finely chiseled face and brilliant twinkling eyes. Her imagination allowed her treacherous body to recall the firm grasp of his hands upon her waist, and she found that her arm actually tingled with the thought of those trailing fingers.

Good lord, Samantha thought, abruptly thrusting the covers aside. *I am certainly fit for Bedlam if I have such thoughts about Edward!*

Since sleep was, for the moment, out of the question, Samantha decided to occupy herself with her manuscript. She rose and found a candle, which she lit from the dying embers in the fireplace and placed on the mahogany writing table. Dipping a pen into the inkwell, she began to write. Her work had not been progressing well of late, possibly because she was nearly burned to the socket from the social whirl. And, as she had not seen Lord Blackwood in a fortnight, she had in truth a certain lack of inspiration for her primary character.

But tonight she willed her mind to conjure up the raven-haired Lord Deverill, whose undeniable attractions were rapidly capturing the affections of the staid and proper Juliana Morriston. Instead, however, Samantha's thoughts drifted in a different direction. To her surprise, Miss Morriston found herself strolling in the park with an old friend from her childhood.

Suddenly an enormous hound came dashing out of nowhere, and Juliana clasped her reticule in dismay. The animal seemed determined to seize upon her as the nearest town substitute for a fox! He began to jump upon her person, and Juliana shrieked in fright and terror.

Her companion, the earl of Edgedown, immediately swung into action. His powerful arms lifted her up and onto a stone wall alongside the graveled path. Then, seemingly from thin air, he pulled out a container of pepper and dashed it down onto the animal's nose. Catapulted into a sneezing frenzy, the stunned creature fled into some bushes, attempting to bury his nose in the dirt. When that failed to bring surcease, he ran in the direction of a nearby lake and was last observed flinging himself into the water.

Juliana could only look on in abject admiration.

"My lord," she said breathlessly, "you have truly saved my life! I am most grateful!"

The earl regarded her with twinkling blue eyes as he reached up to set her down again on solid ground. His hands came around her waist and, as he lifted her, Juliana found her arms resting on his strong shoulders. For a breathless moment their eyes met. Gently he set her down, but his arms remained firmly around her. The earl bent his head to hers and . . .

Disgusted, Samantha threw down her pen. What utter drivel! As if anyone would put such thoughts to paper, and where, for that matter had they come from? Juliana had no business flirting with some *tonnish* earl when she had the Devil Lord firmly in her sights! Samantha pushed her chair back abruptly. This would not do!

The clock chimed one o'clock, its solitary gong a lonely accompaniment to Samantha's bleak spirits. There was not another sound in the house, the family having spent the evening at home and thus retired early. Samantha was certain she was alone in not enjoying the fruits of that beneficial exercise. She grabbed her flannel wrapper and threw it over her thin night rail.

Her door made no sound as it swung on its well-oiled hinges, and Samantha crept into the hallway with her single candle. The corridor was empty, and she quickly made her way to the stairway, her destination the earl's well-stocked library.

On the first floor, she was relieved to see that no servants remained at their posts, a clear sign that the house indeed was sleeping. She turned into the hall leading to the library, only to stop abruptly at the dim light glowing from the open door of the earl's study. Knowing she must pass that door to reach the library, Samantha held her breath in indecision.

Edward was the last person she wished to encounter at this hour! Yet he was clearly still awake. She frowned. She must get herself under control! Perhaps she could even pass quietly by without attracting his notice. She exhaled and began to walk again, carefully shielding her candle.

Suddenly something hard hit her toe, and the impact forced a cry of pain just as the object toppled toward her. Reaching out her arms, she encountered the smooth porcelain of an enormous, heavy vase. The effort to contain the weight left her off balance.

"Drat!" she exclaimed, as her posterior aspect landed with a resounding thump upon the cold, hard marble, her flannel-wrapped body cushioning the vase from the full force of its fall. Her candle fell to the floor, flickered, and extinguished itself.

The folds of her robe had enveloped her legs in a way that—combined with the delicate balancing maneuver necessary to safeguard the vase—left her completely immobile. Her sense of frustration and helplessness was exacerbated when she heard footsteps and looked up to see a large silhouette towering over her in the darkened corridor. The figure vanished for a moment and returned with a candle, which better displayed her awkward predicament for extensive inspection.

"I see you are determined to rid the house of that vase," Edward commented dryly, but made no move toward her. He seemed content, in fact, merely to observe her situation without making any effort to rectify it.

Samantha gave an exasperated sigh.

"It is just like you, Edward, to enjoy my discomfort," she said. "Would it not occur to you, do you think, to help me out of this fix?"

Edward cocked his head and appeared to consider the request. His eyes flicked briefly over her but gave no sign that they registered her awkward dishabille, her flushed face, or the delicate ankles that were more than exposed by the disarray of her garments.

"It is merely that one rarely encounters Samantha Compton in such a helpless pose,'' Edward said amiably, ''that I find I am rather enjoying it.''

At her outraged expression, however, he moved to relieve her of the vase.

''Come, come, Sam! You are not such a poor sport as all that,'' he said briskly. ''Give me your hand and have done.''

Samantha allowed him to help her up, tripping awkwardly into his arms when her foot caught in the folds of her wrapper. Quickly she extricated herself and, blushing, fought for her composure. But by the time she had herself in hand, Edward had returned to his study. Without thinking, she followed him.

He sat at his desk perusing some papers, still attired in immaculate dinner dress, his double-breasted tailcoat and cravat in perfect order. Samantha stood at the doorway uncertainly and after some moments cleared her throat. Edward looked up.

''Still here, Sam?'' he asked, a note of surprise in his voice.

''Yes, that is— See here, Edward, aren't you even going to ask what I was doing prowling about your house in the dead of night?'' she said, perplexed.

A frown crossed his face.

''I assumed you were headed toward the library,'' he said. ''At all events, my house is your house for the nonce. Why should I mind if you prowl about a bit?''

She gave an exasperated sigh, and he looked across his desk at her in concern. Putting his papers aside, he rose and crossed the room to stand at her side.

''Are you not feeling well, my dear? Still got that chill from this morning? You should have been well asleep by now, surely?''

He fixed her with such a look of brotherly solicitousness that Samantha felt like kicking him in the shins, despite the fact that her slippered toes would almost certainly emerge the poorer from contact with his hard-muscled legs. She suppressed the urge but could not suppress a look of irritation.

''There is nothing wrong with me, Edward!'' she said

heatedly. "And I wish you would forget about this morning!"

He smiled and patted her gently on her shoulder. Samantha felt her face flush.

"It shall be as you wish, my dear," he said, turning back to his desk. After a reflective pause, he continued: "You know, Sam, I had not thought you susceptible to the uncertainty of temperament that afflicts most of your sex. In this, perhaps, I was wrong. I can only suggest that perhaps a good book and a good night's sleep will ease your condition."

With that infuriating comment, Edward picked up his quill and began writing.

Samantha stared at him with a look of stunned outrage and promptly spun on her heel, her library mission forgotten.

As she vanished through the door, Edward looked up briefly and then, a faint smile flitting over his face, continued to write.

Chapter 10

❧❧❧❧

By morning, Samantha was ready to dismiss the previous day's madness as the result of her overactive imagination and increasing preoccupation with the fact that her future yet remained to be settled as the Season sped relentlessly past the halfway mark. In such an uncertain climate, it was natural (although lamentable, to be sure) that her mind had found itself in the absurd state of imagining Edward's every gesture and nuance of conversation to be aimed at her and undertaken solely for her benefit.

As for her own startling and rather palpable response to his actions and even, she was forced to acknowledge, his very presence, that perhaps could best be attributed to the fact that her nerves were frayed by the Season's frenzied whirl even as she was experiencing not a small measure of desperation at the paucity of acceptable husband material. That those distressing developments led her to be drawn toward one whose considerable attributes would naturally commend him to any young lady was, perhaps, perfectly understandable.

It was not that there were no acceptable candidates for her hand. There were indeed several gentlemen whose attentions had been flattering and not at all repulsive. Samantha knew she should consider herself most fortunate that a comfortable future for herself and her mother was apparently within her very reach. Unfortunately—and Samantha knew she could not afford the luxury of allowing her thoughts to wander long down this road—none of her suitors moved her in the slightest. None made her heart beat fast or her breath come unsteadily in the startling manner precipitated yesterday by a pair of cobalt eyes and absent-minded caresses.

Coming down the stairs for breakfast, Samantha nearly laughed aloud at the knowledge that her brain had actually duped her into such strange responses over Edward! While he would certainly be the catch of any Season, he was to her only the most amiable of companions, a friend held in the highest affections, certainly, but a friend for all that. Edward had only to crook his finger, after all, to secure any wife he wished; as he had never shown any inclination to take such a precipitous step, there was no chance that he would be turned from his resolute bachelorhood by a snippet of a girl he had known all his life, and indeed had practically raised, if it came to that.

Not that she would wish such a drastic alteration in their relationship. Yet, it was inevitable that matters between them *would* change after her wedding. Almost certainly her marriage would diminish the opportunities for Edward's companionship, for what husband would easily tolerate a wife's easy and familiar friendship with another gentleman? Yet how unhappy such a loss! Their mutual appreciation of the other's mind and spirit went beyond the bonds of a shared childhood. And while friendly verbal sparring often marked their discourse, that, too, was a shared pleasure. Samantha wondered if husbands and wives readily achieved such harmony. Reflecting on the gentlemen she had met this Season, she strongly doubted it.

Could it be then, she mused, pausing on the bottom step much struck by the notion, that what had led her thoughts to take such a turn yesterday was distress over the inevitable loss of that special friendship, and a desire to hold on to it in any form at all? Perhaps that had led her to look at

Edward in a new and unaccustomed light, which, she was happy to say this morning, had completely faded from existence.

Indeed, at breakfast there was little indication that Edward even took note of her existence, a fact that should have given her much reassurance, but which succeeded only in nourishing the tiny seed of anxiety that had begun, inexplicably, to grow in her heart.

He was engaged in polite conversation with Lady Landsdown and Cecelia and offered a cheery greeting to Samantha, but for the most part, he seemed supremely uninterested in any of the ladies' chatter. Indeed, he soon disappeared behind the pages of his newspaper. As this breakfast-time habit was the only apparent social lapse in which Edward had ever indulged, it was treated with complete tolerance and no adverse comment by his female relatives, none of whom seemed to feel the least bit insulted at being so completely ignored.

Samantha stifled an unexpected surge of irritation and concentrated instead on a discussion with Cecelia of the shopping expedition they had planned for that morning. Cecelia was determined to find bishop's blue sarcenet for a new ballgown, even though there were more than enough beautiful creations in her wardrobe. But lately Cecelia had demonstrated an odd dissatisfaction with her appearance and a determination to see each gown more sensational than the last. Samantha wondered if her new mood had anything to do with Lord Formsby, who since their ball had become a frequent caller at Landsdown House but so far had given no indication of the state of his heart.

Samantha would swear that his lordship was more than touched by the fair Cecelia. She suspected that Cecelia returned his regard but was wary of allowing her feelings to progress in the face of Lord Formsby's determined congeniality that, while pleasant enough, stopped short of a lover's ardor. It was most frustrating, Samantha thought. While Cecelia had clearly been pleased at Lord Formsby's gallant solution to her partnerless plight at their ball, and even seemed to Samantha's discerning eye to ponder the matter some days, things clearly had not gone far enough. Perhaps this morning she could learn more from Cecelia, who had so far gently turned away any queries along those lines.

For the time being, it seemed, Lord Formsby was content to divulge nothing about his intentions. In recent days, he had adopted the habit of taking them both around in his carriage in the afternoon, a tactic that neatly avoided creating the impression that he was singling out either lady. Cecelia and Samantha were, as it happened, engaged to go driving with him that very afternoon; the fact of a three-some, of course, would prevent any intimate congress between him and Cecelia.

Something would have to be done, Samantha mused, her mind searching for the possibilities. Her eye lit on Edward. If he could be persuaded to come, it would be perfectly natural for them to pair off, forcing Cecelia and Lord Formsby to deal with each other's company at last. She brushed aside a treacherous thought that it would also give her the opportunity to see if yesterday's madness with Edward could be repeated.

"Edward," Samantha began cheerfully, "would you care to come driving with Cecelia and me this afternoon? I daresay you could persuade Lord Formsby to take us as far as the gravel pits, for he never will, you know. They are not so far beyond the park as all that. It would be a great adventure!"

The earl peered over his paper and frowned.

"Henry is quite right to refuse to take you. I would just as soon not have two ladies under my protection hovering around that desolate spot! 'Tis not safe that far out."

Cecelia joined in. "Perhaps we could merely drive by them, Edward, for you know I have been wishing to visit Nanny Stedham, and she is just a few miles north of there. In her last letter, she said she was not feeling at all the thing."

"Do not try to gammon me, Cecelia. The pits are nearly two miles west of the route to Mrs. Stedham's, which is beyond Paddington, as you well know."

But Samantha was not yet ready to give up. "With two gentlemen we would be perfectly safe. And the change of scenery would be refreshing. Do say we might, Edward!"

But Edward obviously considered the subject closed. He folded his newspaper and pushed back his chair.

"I shall be spending the day at Tattersall's anyway, Sam. I am sure you will manage without me."

Before she could open her mouth to respond, he was gone.

"I could not agree more with your choice, Cecelia! The color very nearly matches your eyes, and the effect is certain to be quite out of the ordinary!" Samantha nodded approvingly at the package that Betsy carried behind them as the two ladies made their way through Leicester Square.

"I hope you are not too fatigued from shopping, Samantha," Cecelia replied, "for I am determined to go this minute to Madame Celeste's. I have a mind to wear the gown at the Assheton ball."

Samantha hurried to keep up with her friend.

"But that is only two days' hence, Cecelia! Surely there are any number of dresses that would suffice. Why, you have not even worn the blush pink Celeste sent last week! You were in raptures over that fabric, as I recall."

"Nevertheless, I shall wear the new blue," Cecelia said in a quiet voice of finality.

Samantha pondered Cecelia's set profile and blushing cheeks. Clearly, there was something afoot. Cecelia had never before needed the boost of a new gown to gain the confidence to face an evening. When they entered the Landsdown town coach, Cecelia made no effort at conversation. Her mouth was pursed in a little frown of worry, and Samantha thought her eyes looked as if she had not been sleeping well. They traveled in silence for a while. Finally Samantha could no longer keep her own counsel.

"Dear friend, I can see that something is troubling you," she began as the carriage rolled to a stop in front of Celeste's little shop. "Although I am reluctant to pry, pray do not mistake my reticence for disregard. If it would help to unburden yourself, I am eager to serve in that capacity, for you must know that you and Edward are my dearest friends!''

If Samantha thought this little speech might have a reassuring effect, she was soon disabused of that notion. Cecelia gave her a long, tragic look and burst into tears.

Samantha's maid, who sat on the cushioned seat across from them, looked at her mistress in awkward distress.

''Betsy, please go and tell John Coachman that we will be a moment longer,'' Samantha ordered, and Betsy scurried out of the carriage.

Samantha pulled out her handkerchief and handed it to Cecelia, who blew her nose and then looked up gratefully, her azure eyes shimmering with tears.

''You must think me a complete watering pot, Samantha! I do apologize for coming undone. I do not know what has happened to me lately. I cannot seem to get through the day without plunging into the most dampening of moods. There is no accounting for it, but there it is.''

Samantha patted Cecelia's arm and fixed her with a steady look.

''Of course you know best, Cecelia, but I happen to believe your troubles can be laid right at the door of one Lord Formsby!''

That statement sent Cecelia into a fresh spasm of tears, and Samantha reached out and hugged her firmly.

''There, there! I have never known you to be such a helpless little mouse, Cecelia! You must recover your spirits and put them to good use! I am persuaded that there is nothing here that cannot be set aright.''

At this bracing speech, Cecelia looked up hopefully and began to dry her eyes with Samantha's handkerchief. The tiny little scrap of linen had quickly ceased being of any use, but Cecelia clutched it fiercely, as if it were a talisman from which she could draw some of Samantha's bolstering optimism.

''You really think so?'' she asked tentatively.

''Of course!'' Samantha replied. ''But you must be frank

with me, Cecelia. You have fallen in love with Lord Formsby, have you not?''

A radiant but tremulous smile shone through the tears.

''I fear it is true, Samantha, but I despair of his affections. Though we are much in his company, he makes no effort to single me out. I am afraid he thinks of me merely as Edward's little sister.''

''Nonsense!'' Samantha retorted. ''I believe that Lord Formsby has indeed tumbled into love, but for reasons of his own is loath to allow you to see it.''

Cecelia's delicate brow furrowed in confusion.

''But why?''

''I do not know for certain, of course. But there are several possible explanations. He may feel that he is no match for the competition—for you are easily the greatest success of the Season.'' Here she frowned. ''But as I do not believe his lordship is so weakhearted, I think we may look elsewhere for the answer.''

Cecelia had forgotten her tears in her fascination with Samantha's theories and eagerly urged her friend on.

''It may be that he does not know his own mind. To be sure, he can only hold you in great esteem,'' Samantha added hastily, seeing Cecelia's face fall, ''but perhaps he wishes to know you better before making a declaration.'' Then she had an inspiration: ''Or perhaps he merely feels awkward openly courting the sister of his best friend! Edward is such a stickler that he may well accept only a paragon for you!''

''I am sure Lord Formsby must be acceptable to any young lady,'' Cecelia said indignantly. ''He moves in the best circles, and his family and fortune are quite acceptable! His conversation is excellent, and his disposition is excessively kind—''

''Yes, well, I am sure you are correct,'' Samantha interrupted to forestall a further litany of Lord Formsby's good qualities. ''And his intentions can only be honorable, but it is obvious that we must do something to get him to come to the point.''

Cecelia frowned doubtfully. ''I have tried to encourage

him, but we are never private together! All these drives in the park are worse than nothing—it is always the three of us and—oh!'' Cecelia broke off in horrified embarrassment. ''I beg your pardon, Samantha! I did not mean anything by that!''

Far from being offended, Samantha laughed merrily. ''Goose! You do but echo my own thoughts! That is why I attempted to persuade Edward to come with us this afternoon, thinking that it would give you and Lord Formsby a few moments without my chattering presence. But as usual, your brother refused to cooperate. Perhaps I could come down with the headache this afternoon!''

''Do you think that is a bit obvious?'' Cecelia replied doubtfully.

Samantha shook her head. ''I am certain he would welcome the opportunity to be alone with you, as he did at our ball,'' Samantha said, as Cecelia's eyes widened in sudden understanding.

''I knew you never felt faint a day in your life, Samantha! How daring of you!'' Cecelia exclaimed. ''I see I am in your debt for a most enjoyable waltz.'' Her face flushed with the memory, but quickly fell. ''It did seem as though there was . . . a regard in his eyes when he looked at me, but then the dance ended, and he was gone,'' she said, her melodic voice tinged with remembered sadness.

''This time,'' Samantha said firmly, ''we shall not let him slip the hook.''

Oblivious of the forces at work on his behalf, Lord Formsby raised the bronze knocker at Landsdown House shortly before five in the afternoon and was promptly ushered into the blue parlor off the marbled foyer. His solitude was allowed to persist for about ten minutes before the door opened and Cecelia entered. She was attired in a deep blue carriage dress and a fetching bonnet that was trimmed in a pleated ribbon in the same dramatic shade of blue that emphasized her startling blue eyes.

Formsby looked at the door expectantly, but only Cecelia stood there. He made a belated bow.

"Good afternoon, Lady Cecelia," he said formally.

Cecelia crossed the room and perched delicately upon a divan.

"Samantha is not yet ready, I am afraid," she said.

She patted the divan, and he looked at it doubtfully before settling on an adjacent upholstered leather chair. Cecelia's jaw tightened in frustration, but her face remained serene.

"I am happy to have a moment for us to speak privately, Lord Formsby," Cecelia began. "I have not thanked you properly for rescuing me at our ball last week."

Formsby shifted in his chair, but his eyes never left Cecelia's face. "Doubtless, any number of gentlemen would have done the same had they but noticed your plight," he replied uneasily.

"Come, Lord Formsby," Cecelia said, and leaned forward to fix him with an earnest look. She rested her hand lightly on his arm. "I am persuaded that few gentlemen have your sensibility of the needs of others. But I see I am causing you discomfort," she added quickly, as an embarrassed frown crossed his features. She leaned back on the divan suddenly with a weary expression.

"Lady Cecelia, I fear you are unwell," Formsby said in alarm. "I shall summon help at once!" He rose to move toward the door, but Cecelia clung to his arm.

"No!" she said, and clutched his arm tighter. "I am not unwell. Merely in need of some moral support, I fear . . ."

She let these words trail off; but while Formsby looked at her with curious concern, he was too well mannered to question her about what clearly appeared to be a private matter.

After a moment Cecelia sighed and leaned back, her hand still on his arm.

"Lord Formsby, you will forgive me if I unburden myself to you, but as I know you to be a great friend to our family, I feel I can take you into my confidence." She closed her eyes, and he stared, fascinated, at the delicate shadows her eyelashes cast upon her pale skin.

"I hope, Lady Cecelia, that you may always count me as your friend," he said at last.

Cecelia stared at the steady brown eyes and took a deep breath.

"You see, Lord Formsby, Edward has some strange notions about the man he wishes me to choose for a husband," Cecelia said.

His brows rose sharply, but he said nothing.

"He is all that one could wish for in a brother, of course, and is excessively understanding of my wishes. But I fear that he is trying to force me—perhaps that is too strong a word—to persuade me, I should say, to marry a man I cannot like at all!"

At this dramatic declaration, Formsby's breath drew in sharply.

"Edward? I cannot think it! Why, surely you must be free to marry where you will!" he said, and the urgency of his tone gave Cecelia's heart hope.

With the steely control worthy of one of the crown's best generals, Cecelia removed her hand from his arm. She opened her eyes wide and looked into his concerned face.

"It is a matter of some delicacy, my lord, and I wonder if it is fair to burden you with it."

His hand moved to cover hers and gave it a firm, reassuring squeeze.

"Ought to allow me to make that decision," Lord Formsby said quietly.

The smile Cecelia bestowed upon him was dazzling. Quickly she continued. "You see, Edward has the oddest notion that he wishes me to marry one of his friends," she said.

Cecelia did not so much glance in Lord Formsby's direction during the stunned silence that greeted that pronouncement

"Edward trusts so few people," she continued, "that he refuses . . . well, he has discouraged me from accepting any suitors with whom he cannot claim a longstanding acquaintance. But I am afraid that the one who has asked permission to pay his addresses is a gentleman I can hold in no regard! He is pleasant enough, but I am afraid he lacks a certain . . . kindness. I do not mean that he is cruel, at least if he is I would not know it until afterward, you understand.''

Lord Formsby had been unable to disguise his growing horror at this speech and more than once looked as if he wished to gather the brave Lady Cecelia into his arms.

''Who is this beast Edward is forcing upon you?'' he demanded.

''Oh, but I cannot reveal that, my lord, as I am sure you understand. The matter is not settled yet.''

She modestly withdrew her hand and looked shyly into his face, hoping that Samantha had not overreached in devising this tale. But the fact that he had appeared to accept her story bolstered Samantha's argument that his judgment would be clouded by his feelings for her.

Lord Formsby's frown deepened.

''I shall take it up with him at the first opportunity. When he knows how great is your upset, I am sure . . .''

''No!'' Cecelia cried. ''You must not say a word to him, my lord! He is stubborn enough to become even more entrenched in his view. Please promise you will say nothing! I would not have given you my confidences, sir, if I had thought you would take them forthwith to Edward!''

Formsby looked down into her pleading face, clearly unequal to the task of disappointing her.

''Very well, Lady Cecelia, I will say nothing. But something must be done. You cannot be forced to marry a man you do not admire,'' he said forcefully, fixing her with a determined gaze.

There was at that moment a knock followed by the entrance of Lord Landsdown's butler.

''I beg your pardon, Lady Cecelia,'' Petersham said, ''Miss Compton sends word that she has the headache and cannot join you this afternoon.''

''Thank you.'' Cecelia said quickly and turned to Formsby. ''It is unfortunate, my lord, that we are not to have Samantha's company this afternoon.''

She lowered her eyes and then looked up again shyly.

"Perhaps it is not too great a burden, sir, if you are still willing, to take me up with you?"

His lordship stared at her azure eyes, sinking into their extraordinary depths.

"I should be honored, Lady Cecelia," he said, and offered his arm.

Chapter 11

Edward was an uncommonly good dancer, Samantha decided, watching him carefully out of the corner of her eye as he executed the figures of the quadrille with Lady Alynn. She herself was being partnered by Lord Fitzwilliam, whose own abilities were more than adequate. Still, Samantha found herself thinking that Edward cut quite a dash on the dance floor.

His attire was always elegantly correct, of course, but this evening he displayed to perfection in a brilliantly tailored black evening coat, white waistcoat, snugly fitting pantaloons, and patterned silk stockings. His snowy white cravat was tied in a splendid style that Samantha guessed was his own creation. It had drawn the admiring eyes of quite a few young bucks, and she knew it would soon appear in ballrooms all over London.

He had signed her card for the next dance, and Samantha found to her irritation that she could not suppress her anticipation, even though the dance was to be the minuet, which she usually found tedious. But to her surprise, when he came to claim her hand, he suggested a turn in the viscountess Assheton's gardens. She felt momentarily disappointed, at least until she felt his firm hand at her back guide her to the stone walkways that had been laid out in a seemingly desultory fashion. Suddenly the evening had taken on a magical air that in no way was dispelled by what followed.

"I much prefer the quiet solitude of this setting," he began, one hand idly flicking away a thin branch that intruded as they strolled. "It is so much easier to converse and enjoy the company of one's companion. Do you not agree?"

Samantha looked over at his fine profile.

"Of course," was all she could think to say.

He seemed lost in reflection, but finally he turned to her, his face wearing the preoccupied half smile of one whose thoughts are far away.

"Do you remember those evenings at the pond," he asked softly, "when we would go swimming under the stars? I am quite sure your mother would have forbidden it. You never did tell her, did you?"

She was taken aback. What had possessed him to bring that up? She couldn't have been eight and he barely twelve when they had begun their summertime habit of meeting at night to wash off the heat of the day in the pond near the Compton property line. She blushed at the thought of how skimpy were the garments in which they swam—an old chemise for her, a pair of breeches for him. It was nothing to them then, of course. They were just children, and these strange undercurrents that now flared between them had not been present then. He was correct that her mother would have been greatly distressed at the knowledge, but in those days there was no one to notice her absence, as Lady Compton remained in her bed and Sir Harry was customarily off on one of his sprees. The nurserymaids her father had hired for her care were not particularly diligent, often displaying a fondness for spirits or other unwholesome diversions such that Samantha frequently had the nights to herself, which suited her perfectly.

Their evening swim had been one of those secret, magical rituals of childhood that had nourished the seed that gave rise to her rich imagination. After their swim, they would lie on the ground looking up at the stars. Edward would point out the constellations, and Samantha would spin stories about them. Summer after summer they had passed the evenings that way, until one summer Edward did not come to the pond. The hurt, a child's hurt, had been devastating. They had never discussed it.

"No, I never told her," Samantha admitted, surprised at the pain that tore anew at her heart across the years. "But anyway, you stopped coming."

Edward caught the tiny tremble of her mouth.

"You understood why?" he asked quietly.

"No," she said, unable to keep the hurt from her voice. "Although I suppose I do now. You just grew up."

He took her hand and rubbed it between his. The warmth traveled up her arm and down into the pit of her stomach.

"Yes," he said, fixing her with a steady gaze. "And I knew you would, too, someday. It is not at all the thing for a young man to take a barely dressed young lady swimming at night, Sam. Childhood does not last forever."

She heard the wistful note in his voice and something else she could not name. She smiled nervously and looked up to find him regarding her with an impenetrable expression.

"Yes, I know that," she said lightly. "But sometimes I wish it would."

"I do not."

Samantha felt the arm tighten about her waist. She stared, mesmerized, as he studied her face for a long, endless moment. Gently he leaned down and planted a chaste kiss on her forehead.

"I believe I hear the music ending," he said softly. "It is time to return you to your next partner."

Lady Darrow chewed nervously on her generous lower lip. Her quarry, the earl of Landsdown, was but a few feet away, conversing with one of his friends.

The smile she had pasted on her face was a game attempt to hide her nervousness. Her color was unusually high, even for one accustomed to subtly heightening such effect with her paint boxes. One delicate fingernail had been gnawed nearly to the quick, and her pulse beat so forcefully that anyone whose eyes lingered over her swanlike neck could not miss its throbbing.

It had not gone so well, this plan of Blackwood's. Her attempts had been too oblique—arranging for the breakdown of her carriage one day near Astley's, as well as other encounters that had appeared to occur at the behest of chance. The earl had parried all her efforts, acknowledging her politely but with a slight chill that told her he was not interested in pursuing the matter further.

Blackwood was eager to make his move with the Compton chit, however, and this time she must arrange a distraction that would effectively remove Landsdown's protection from Miss Compton for as long as Blackwood required it. She took a deep breath and straightened her skirts. She was still quite a striking woman, her blond hair carefully arranged to evoke an air of abandon, and her rather ample charms carefully displayed in the most tastefully daring gowns that her modiste could create. Moreover, her appearance and demeanor bespoke not only an awareness of her attractions, but also an acknowledgment of how the game was played. Many men found that a devastating combination.

Edward, however, was another matter altogether. Complicating things was the fact that she was, in the tiniest corner of her heart, perhaps still a little in love with him, at least as much as she allowed herself to experience such an unselfish emotion. Thus his rejection, offered with such chilling politeness, stung to the core of her jaded soul.

And so, when Lady Darrow approached the earl of Landsdown at the Assheton ball, she gritted her teeth and braced herself for a cool reception.

"My lord, I fear I am in need of your assistance," she began, gently placing her fingertips on his arm—but there was no warmth in the piercing blue eyes that turned to her.

"Good evening, Catharine," Edward responded, his voice flat. Then, more softly: "How may I be of service? Another carriage breakdown or something else altogether? An escort, perhaps, unable to take you home?"

Edward's friend, Lord Fitzwilliam, was staring in obvious curiosity. Lady Darrow consigned him to the devil with a pointed look of dismissal. He coughed awkwardly and excused himself. A pair of dancers swirled nearby, their gay laughter a strange counterpoint to this little encounter.

"Perhaps, my lord, we can go somewhere a little more private?" Lady Darrow suggested. When he remained immobile, she tugged on his sleeve and whispered urgently: "Please, Edward, even you cannot wish me to so completely humble myself as to beg for a moment of your time."

One eyebrow arched upward. Finally he gave a slight nod and allowed her to lead him down a corridor to a small parlor.

She moved to sit on an intimate little settee, but if she had hoped Edward would join her there, she was mistaken. The earl leaned carelessly against the mantel half a room away, content, it seemed, to wait for her to speak.

Lady Darrow bit her lip and clutched her fan, and found she could not meet the look of disdain she saw in his face.

"Oh, Edward!" she said finally, rising to close the distance between them, "if you only knew how much I have suffered!"

As this comment elicited only a barely perceptible elevation of one eyebrow, Lady Darrow promptly burst into tears.

Edward looked at the forlorn figure and sighed. After a moment he pulled a piece of snowy white linen from the pocket of his tailcoat and offered it to her.

"Quite a performance, my dear, but as I have no notion yet what is causing you such suffering, the effect, I'm afraid, is quite lost," Edward said, an edge of impatience evident in his voice.

Lady Darrow blew her nose into the handkerchief. When she spoke, her voice held a curious note of dignity.

"You cannot be so lost to all feeling toward me, Edward, that you do not care or wonder at the misfortune that has befallen me," she said, dabbing her nose with his handkerchief.

"As to the first statement, Catharine, you signaled quite

clearly years ago that my feeling is of no interest to you. As to the second, I am not aware of any such misfortune, although I have the strong impression that you are about to enlighten me.''

The only response to this was a renewed bout of tears, but as that produced no reaction whatsoever, Lady Darrow angrily looked up into his impassive face.

''I own that I once wronged you, Edward, but that is no reason for you to treat me with less consideration than one of your servants! I can only say I am sorry you have turned into such a poor specimen as to make sport out of one who has fallen on unhappy times!''

She turned away from him so that he could not see her face. The silence in the room stretched for several minutes as Edward stared at her back.

Her angry words had found their mark. Now that the shell surrounding his heart had been pricked by a young lady with chestnut hair and mesmerizing hazel eyes, he found his carefully crafted veneer was no longer so immune to the feelings of others.

And that was perhaps why Edward was not, in fact, devoid of pity when he pondered Catharine Darrow's trembling shoulders.

So while he would have, not so long ago, abruptly turned and left the room, now his hands moved tentatively to embrace her in a gesture intended to give comfort. She quickly nestled deeply into the warmth of his embrace.

They were locked in this touching pose as Samantha and Cecelia opened the parlor door, intent on private discussion. The shock of such a discovery left both young ladies rooted to the threshold. Lady Darrow smiled demurely. Edward's eyes traveled instantly to Samantha's face, which had frozen in an unguarded expression of dismay. Cecelia recovered first, smiling as if there were nothing at all odd about the situation.

''Do forgive us, Lady Darrow, Edward,'' she said briskly. ''We had no notion that this room was occupied.''

And with that, she turned and made a swift and efficient exit, pulling the silent Samantha along.

Lady Darrow looked hesitantly up at Edward, whose eyes lingered on the door, burning with a strange expression. Quickly she spoke. "It is obvious that we cannot be private here, Edward. May I be so bold as to ask if you might call on me tomorrow afternoon?" she said, and her voice carried a pleading note.

Edward hesitated, and she buried her face in his chest.

"I would not ask it, Edward, only I must unburden myself to someone. Pray do not deny me this," she said quietly.

The earl looked down at the top of her head and felt her warm body pressed against him. He shook his head but heard his voice answer, "Very well, Catharine, I shall come to you at four."

She swept out of the room. Edward stared at the open door, but all he could see was the horrified expression on Samantha's face.

Cecelia chattered rapidly as the ladies made their way back to the main ballroom.

"I had no notion Edward and Lady Darrow were . . . together again," she said. "I cannot say I am pleased about it, but of course Edward will do what he will. I hope he is not considering bringing her into the family, though! She is really not the sort I would care to call sister! Indeed, if the stories about her are to be believed, I should think Edward's notion of propriety would not let him entertain such a thought. She is rumored to have scores of lovers, you know. Well, who knows where love will lead one?"

Samantha said nothing but found Cecelia's words troubling. In fact, the scene she had witnessed had profoundly shaken her, though she could not precisely say why. The sight of Edward holding Lady Darrow in his arms had sent a shiver of alarm through her. She shook her head in confusion, mystified at her feelings. Of course Edward would eventually marry, just as she would. He was sought after by many ladies, and it was only natural to assume that one day one of them would succeed where others had failed. So why did the thought—and sight—of Edward embracing

Lady Darrow upset her? Moreover, she felt something akin to anger, as if he had betrayed her.

"I wanted to seek your counsel in the matter of Lord Formsby," Cecelia was saying anxiously. "I fear our plan is not working! Although he immediately signed my dance card when first we arrived, I have not seen him since. Often at such occasions he is bound to engage one in amiable conversation, but tonight it seems he cannot abide me! I am certain he signed my card only to be polite! Oh, I wish I had worn the blush pink gown after all!"

"Nonsense, Cecelia! The blue made up as beautifully as we could have imagined!" Samantha retorted, determined to purge her mind of any thought of Edward or Lady Darrow. "You are simply at loose ends because Lord Formsby is the first man who has not fallen all over himself to win your affections. I'll wager you will sing a different tune before this evening is out! If I am not mistaken, here comes his lordship now!"

Cecelia gave a sharp intake of breath as she saw the approaching figure, whose face bore an unusually determined look.

He bowed when he reached the ladies and then directed his gaze to Cecelia.

"B'lieve I have the honor of this dance, Lady Cecelia, but I wonder if we may forego it in order to speak privately?"

His face was grave as Cecelia extended her hand. He tucked it into his arm and led her away from the dancers to a small niche off the main ballroom.

Lord Formsby was troubled. He could no longer deny to himself that his initial attraction to Lady Cecelia had blossomed into something far stronger. His reluctance to declare himself derived in part from an indecision of strategy, for he had no wish to join the throng of her fawning suitors, each more fatuous than the last. Moreover, he admitted to an uncertainty about the lady's own inclinations. And so he had played a game of cat and mouse, seeking out opportunities to bask in her company but avoiding those that would give rise to speculation either on

Cecelia's part or on her brother's. But because his was a loving nature that yearned to bestow love unhesitatingly and have it returned in equal measure, Lord Formsby was finding it increasingly difficult to keep up the charade.

This latest wrinkle had thrown his thoughts into chaos. He did not want to believe that Edward could be so unfeeling toward his sister as to force her into a union she did not want. Indeed, Formsby had some idea of the reasons behind Edward's carefully cultivated aloofness and did not think his friend would go so far as to extend such treatment to his own family. Yet there was Cecelia's testimony, and he could not ignore it.

In addition, he had the evidence of his own eyes. Twice this evening she had danced with Edward's friend Fitzwilliam, who was known to enjoy great success with the fairer sex. In fact, that gentleman had held Cecelia particularly close during a waltz, to Lord Formsby's great distress. It must be Fitz whom Edward had in mind for her! Formsby could imagine the mistresses Fitz would keep on the side, the flirtations he would set up with married ladies looking for someone more interesting than their husbands— all the while Cecelia would be forced to bear his children and bravely endure such treatment as all of society winked knowingly. He shuddered at the thought of such a life for her.

And so Lord Formsby had decided on a course of action, that, while it did not commit him irrevocably, placed him in a position to rescue the fair Cecelia from such a fate.

"I have a proposition, Lady Cecelia, that I hope may help you rid Edward of his ill-conceived notion," he began.

Cecelia felt a surge of exhilaration and privately congratulated Samantha on her insight. But then she heard his next words, which was not the proposition she had hoped for.

"Deuced awkward—hope you won't be offended," he stammered loudly, his face flushed as if with exertion.

Alarmed at the sound of his voice, he lowered it to barely a whisper, so that Cecelia was forced to incline her head to him in order to hear. He continued in a halting voice but with a rather fierce look on his face:

"No reason why you must marry anyone merely because he is your brother's friend, but as long as that remains Edward's wish, I think we may satisfy him by . . . pretending to be engaged in a . . . courtship of our own."

Here Lord Formsby reddened, and Cecelia felt a wave of dejection overtake her. She schooled her features into a mask of calm serenity, however.

"But this is interesting beyond measure, Lord Formsby," she said politely. "Pray, do continue."

He looked around the terrace to make certain they would not be overheard.

"Thought perhaps that if I called on you, you know, for outings and took you around—just the two of us now, without Miss Compton, although she is delightful company, to be sure . . ."

"Indeed," murmured Cecelia.

". . . that Edward would think I was, that is, that my intentions were . . ." He left off, momentarily at a loss.

"Honorable?" Cecelia offered helpfully.

"Just so!" Lord Formsby said, brightening. "If Edward thought I was paying my addresses, well, one friend is as good as another for his sister, I'll warrant. This way, he ain't likely to press you to accept Fitz!"

"Fitz?" she echoed uncertainly.

"Lord Fitzwilliam. Oh, I know you can't say anything, but I know what I have seen with my own eyes, Lady Cecelia," he said confidently.

Cecelia looked up at the brown eyes that were burning with intense fervor at his plan, and wondered what it would be like to have them look at her with a warmth generated by an entirely different feeling. His friendly smile exuded kindness, but kindness was not what she sought. She was tempted to abandon the whole effort. Only, if there were a chance it would work . . .

"Lord Formsby, your idea is most gallant. I accept your proposal—proposition," she quickly amended, fluttering her fan. "There is just one thing."

He waited expectantly.

"Have you thought what might occur if my brother

actually demands to know your intentions? Surely he must, if such a charade long continues. What then? In performing the noble office of extricating me from the unwanted attentions of one gentleman, you ought not to place yourself into a position wherein you feel yourself obligated to offer for me."

Formsby's eyes widened. She had given voice to a thought that nagged in the back of his mind when he devised this scheme.

"Don't think it will come to that, Lady Cecelia," he parried.

"But we would do well to consider such an outcome," she persisted.

Placing her hand lightly on his sleeve, she fixed him with a look of solicitousness. When she spoke, her tone was sweet sincerity itself.

"For that matter, I certainly do not wish to see the acting out of this scheme place upon you the burden of finding yourself overmuch in my company."

Lord Formsby bowed gallantly and ventured to bring her hand to his lips.

"Won't be a hardship," he said somberly.

Cecelia supposed she must make do with that.

Samantha normally enjoyed dancing with Lord Fitzwilliam, as he was a most attractive and highly eligible gentleman. Indeed, the eyes of many eager young ladies often followed them when they were on the dance floor, and she had to admit that his combination of reddish hair and green eyes was devastating. His wit was considerable, and she found she vastly preferred his company to many of the young bucks who scribbled their names on her card.

But tonight she was so preoccupied that she was forced to apologize to him for her inattentiveness during their second dance. He gave her a reassuring smile before turning her over to her next partner. She went through the motions with half a dozen partners before she found, to her relief, an empty spot on her dance card.

She deliberately moved away from the chairs in which

the group of chaperons that included Lady Landsdown was sitting. She wanted to be alone with her thoughts. The strange and spellbinding turn in the garden with Edward had given the evening a special air, but that was before the affecting scene in the parlor with Lady Darrow. Samantha knew a sense of dread at the thought of confronting him again after that awkward encounter and was grateful, at least, that he was not signed up for another dance.

She wandered past a bay window and gratefully sank onto the cushioned window seat. Through the glass she could see the full moon had bathed the rooftops and chimneys of London in its light. The town looked beautiful, she realized. Then why did it suddenly seem to her a forlorn and empty place?

A light touch on her elbow interrupted her thoughts, and she turned to find herself the subject of scrutiny by Lord Blackwood.

"I do hope I am not disturbing you, Miss Compton," he said in a velvety voice.

Her mind registered the vaguely menacing demeanor, penetrating black eyes, and imposing brows, but the effect somehow did not release her from her listless and dejected state.

"Lord Blackwood," Samantha acknowledged politely. "We have not seen much of you this fortnight. I trust you have been well?"

A rough bark of a laugh told her what he thought of the question, but as if to meliorate its effect, Blackwood reached out and brought her hand gallantly to his lips.

"That I have been deprived of your company, Miss Compton, must be charged to unfortunate happenstance. We appear to move in slightly different circles, and as I have not been encouraged to call upon you, it follows that we must, of necessity, find ourselves much apart," he said, giving her hand a squeeze.

Samantha brought herself to attention then, not entirely liking the direction in which this conversation was headed. Her suspicions were confirmed a moment later.

"I can remedy that situation, my dear," he said softly

into her ear, "were you to grant me the privilege of taking you driving tomorrow afternoon."

"Lord Blackwood, I do not think Landsdown would precisely encourage such an outing," she said frankly, eschewing the temptation to plead another engagement.

He smiled enigmatically.

"I believe your vigilant earl will be otherwise engaged tomorrow afternoon and is likely not to remark upon your absence," he said with a smirk. "Lady Darrow has confided to me that he intends to call at her house. They are longstanding . . . friends, you know."

The seed of anger that had been planted at the sight of Edward and Lady Darrow's embrace suddenly came to full fruition, and Samantha felt her head throb.

"Edward's plans are no concern of mine, my lord," she said in a clipped voice. "You mistake the situation if you think I allow my choice of companions and activities to be dictated by Lord Landsdown's preferences. You may call for me at half past four."

With that, she spun on her heel, not knowing whether the blazing anger she felt was directed at Blackwood or at Edward. Not that it mattered, of course, for she was persuaded the entire male species left much to be desired.

Blackwood, meanwhile, watched her determined flight with great satisfaction.

Chapter 12

As the Assheton ball had gone on until quite early in the morning, Samantha did not expect to see anyone when she came down for breakfast. Cecelia was still abed, having kept Samantha awake until an unconscionable hour with an account of Lord Formsby's plan to save her from Edward's ruthless dictates, such account being punctuated by many expressions of frustrations and anxiety on that young lady's part. Lady Landsdown, eschewing the notion that ladies of the *ton* do not show their face until noon, was accustomed to taking an early breakfast. But this morning she, too, apparently was feeling the need to recover lost sleep.

Samantha had endured a restless night and, ever an early riser at all events, had not been able to keep to her chamber once the sun was up. She had, however, every expectation of dining alone this morning, since there was no reason at all for any of the members of the Landsdown household to be below at this early hour.

"Good morning, Sam," said a deep baritone as she entered the breakfast parlor, startling her into a tiny shriek.

"Edward! I might have known you would attempt to scare me out of my skin!" Samantha responded, and she was certain that the edge in her voice did not mask her

confusion and embarrassment at having to face him so soon
after last night. Indeed, while he calmly sipped his coffee,
all she could envision was the close embrace in which he
held the beautiful Lady Darrow, his lips lightly resting
against the top of that lady's hair. Samantha was certain that
he could read her face, and so she carefully avoided meeting
his eyes. But he gave no hint that he noticed her discompo-
sure.

"As it is my house, I cannot imagine why my presence in
it should prove startling in the least," Edward said, returning to the plate of ham he was demolishing quite successfully.

At that, Samantha walked briskly over to the sideboard
and began to fill her plate, waving off the footman who
hovered attentively. Her hands were unsteady, and she kept
her back to the table so Edward would not see.

"It is merely that I did not expect to see anyone up yet,
since we returned home so late," Samantha said, her voice
elaborately casual.

"Oh, I am never one to remain abed in the morning.
Some country habits are hard to shake, as I expect you
know," he replied amiably. "But in truth, I did not sleep
well last night and finally, at dawn's light, consigned the
attempt to perdition."

Samantha turned and looked at him fully for the first
time. His face bore none of the shadows and lines that she
was certain hers now possessed after a restless night. There
were no circles under his eyes, no obvious signs of the sleep
he had lost. Still, she thought she detected a tightening
around the mouth, a slight tension in his usually smooth
face, and she wondered at the cause of it. She hesitated, and
then, as the footman left the room, decided to cast caution to
the wind. This was Edward, after all, and he had brought the
matter up himself.

"I confess to some difficulty sleeping also," she said
lightly. "I suppose those new quadrilles were simply
whirling endlessly in my head." He said nothing, and so she
continued: "But was there anything particular that kept you
from your rest, if I may inquire?"

"That is indeed very bold of you, impudent child," Edward replied with the trace of a smile. He was pleased to see her relax somewhat, although he wondered at her continuing distress. His instincts told him that she was still troubled by the encounter she had stumbled upon last night, and the reasons for her reaction he would have dearly liked to explore with her further.

But no, it was too early in the game. Nor could he confide in her the true reason for his sleeplessness, for it would be folly to confess that he had lain abed for hours haunted by the look on her face when she had discovered him with Catharine. Folly to let her suspect that he envisioned holding her in Catharine's stead, and disastrous even to hint at what he had imagined they would do in such a circumstance.

Instead, he smoothed some butter on a biscuit and took a bite. "I expect, Sam, you must allow a gentleman's nocturnal meanderings to remain his own, else you will get the worst sort of reputation. Suffice it to say that in pondering some unresolved matters, I allowed my brain to exert itself sufficiently so as to effectively preclude that state most conducive to sleep. A silly habit that often plagues us humans, but there you have it."

He allowed his eye to rove over the newspaper next to his plate.

Samantha gave an exasperated sigh.

"Edward, what is it you find so interesting in that infernal newspaper?"

"Marbles," he replied.

"I beg your pardon?" She looked up, a perplexed frown wrinkling her features.

"Surely you know of Lord Elgin's marbles, my dear. They are, after all, a favorite target of your Lord Byron."

"He is not *my* Lord Byron, Edward! But of course, it is no secret whom Byron meant by 'Athena's Scottish plunderer,'" she said. "But what has that to say about anything?"

Edward smiled indulgently.

"It is quite clear, Sam, that your awareness of the events

that have plunged London into such turmoil is nonexistent. I assume that can be laid at the door of your all-consuming social schedule, but really, my dear, for one who calls herself an artist, you display an alarming lack of concern for the fate of the works of others of your stamp.''

''I am not that manner of artist, Edward! Merely a fledgling writer. Although I confess that, Lord Byron notwithstanding, it would be a pity to see England deprived of the treasure of such priceless sculpture.''

''Especially as such priceless treasure has nothing to do with our ancestors but everything to do with those of the Greeks!'' Edward retorted. ''But at all events, I collect you would agree with Mr. Haydon, whose attack on those who would devalue the marbles is in all of the newspapers and should go far in establishing his reputation.''

Samantha took up some of the newspaper and was silent as she read.

''Oh, but this is marvelous, Edward!'' she declared, and began to read aloud: '' 'There are some men who have that hateful propensity of sneering at all which the world holds high, sacred or beautiful; not with the view of dissipating doubt, or giving the delightful comfort of conviction, but to excite mysterious belief of their own sagacity, to cloak their own envy, to chuckle if they can confuse, and revel if they can chill the feelings: according to them love is nothing but lust; religion is nothing but delusion; all high views and elevated notions, wild dreams and distempered fancies.' ''

She could not suppress a blush at that last, but shook her head finally, laughing: ''What person had the misfortune of incurring this gentleman's wrath? For I declare, his barbs must sting indeed when they find their mark.''

''Why, his target is the inestimable Mr. Payne Knight, whose supercilious testimony before the Commons' Select Committee did much to depress Lord Elgin's hope that the government would purchase his treasures. According to that gentleman, the marbles are only of the second rank.''

Samantha was watching him, a thoughtful look on her face.

"I had no notion, Edward, that you were interested in antiquities," she said.

His laugh had a slightly bitter edge. "I collect that you would join the rest of society in believing that my chief interests lie in achieving the perfect mathematical, or perhaps inventing a new style of cravat that will proliferate in triumph through drawing rooms all over London," he said, and his eyes were hard.

Samantha colored, remembering her own thoughts last night about that very subject. Edward's eyes narrowed as he observed her reaction.

"Do I detect that the country miss has become so captivated by the *ton* that she has decided to accept its view as her own?"

Samantha shook her head, surprised by the sudden unpleasant turn of the conversation. "Nay, Edward. As you well know, I have never accepted the truth of that exquisitely inaccessible image you persist in presenting to the world," she retorted. "Nor do I know why you are at great pains to create such an impression. I confess, I have often wondered about the cause of it. There was a time, I am persuaded, when the world found you much more approachable, and you cared not a fig for the cut of your coat."

Edward was silent for so long that Samantha dropped her eyes, wondering if she had deeply offended him with her frankness. She shifted in her seat and finally dared to look over at her breakfast companion.

He was studying her with such an unfathomable expression that Samantha wanted to avert her eyes again, but somehow she could not. A strange current passed between them. The ticking of the clock over the mantel suddenly seemed deafening, and Samantha felt her palms grow moist. It was happening again, she realized, this strange and unsettling sensation she felt in Edward's presence. It was most uncomfortable. And yet, as she felt herself pulled into the oddly intense expression that burned in Edward's deep blue eyes, she found she could not speak or move. The moment hung between them.

Suddenly Edward rose.

"Would you like to see the marbles, Sam?" His casual tone was at odds with the strange message in his eyes.

Samantha stared, dazed.

"See . . . them?" she asked, haltingly.

"Yes. They are in the damp and dusty courtyard at Burlington House, out of the public eye for the nonce while Lord Cavendish refurbishes his new home. But George is a particular acquaintance of mine, and I might be able to arrange a private viewing. You would be the envy of all of London, my dear, since it is likely to be months before they can be set up for public viewing at the museum, if indeed Parliament agrees to purchase them."

Samantha managed a smile.

"Why, that sounds like quite an adventure, Edward! I should be delighted."

"I warn you, many of the sculptures are not precisely proper viewing for a delicately bred society miss," he said as he turned to leave the room.

A devilish look danced in her hazel eyes. "I am sure I do not know anyone here fitting that description, Edward, do you?" she asked with elaborate innocence.

"Perhaps not," he said, and his smile robbed the words of their sting and sent her heart into her throat.

As Lord Blackwood had foretold, Edward was not at home when he came to collect her that afternoon. Cecelia and Lady Landsdown were paying calls without her, as Samantha had pleaded the excuse of a headache. There was thus no one to raise any difficulty when Blackwood appeared at the door, although Samantha thought she imagined just the slightest frown of disapproval on Petersham's face.

But when she skipped down the steps and beheld Blackwood's equipment, she stopped in dismay.

"But a closed carriage, my lord!" she protested. "You must know that Lady Landsdown would not countenance my driving off with you in such a conveyance. I had best go and fetch my maid." She turned toward the house, where Petersham still hovered at the open door.

''Nonsense, Miss Compton! I am persuaded that Lady Landsdown would not wish you to get a drenching, and that is just what would happen if we went in my new cabriolet, if I haven't misjudged that sky. Besides, you see my coachman at the reins,'' he said smoothly. ''I do hope you do not think me of such poor character as to take advantage of a lady.''

Samantha stared at the carriage doubtfully.

''It is not that, my lord, but rather that I have no wish to call into question the excellence of Lady Landsdown's chaperonage by having her friends observe us so conveyed,'' she said.

''Then we shall just have to choose a route where Lady Landsdown's friends are not likely to find themselves,'' Blackwood said congenially, gently holding her elbow and nudging her toward the carriage.

When she hesitated still, he added: ''I had not thought the original Miss Compton so bound by society's dictates. Indeed, it was but last evening that you so fervently declared your independence, I believe.''

Samantha shot him an annoyed look and stepped into the carriage.

Edward, meanwhile, found himself standing stiffly in the private sitting room that adjoined Lady Darrow's bedchamber, as that lady reclined rather delicately on a gold brocade divan, her form draped in a flimsy pink robe that made only a pretense of its ostensible function of assuring its wearer a proper degree of modesty.

He was disgusted at himself for having been manipulated into such a situation, but it had come upon him before he realized it. When he had called, Lady Darrow's housekeeper had quickly shown him up the stairs and into the chamber, murmuring something about her mistress having the headache but being most firm that she must see him that day. He was ushered into the sitting room and found, to his dismay, the object of his call displayed rather provocatively before his eyes.

''What is this nonsense, Catharine?'' the earl demanded

sternly. "I came here in kindness to hear your troubles, only to find you have arranged yourself like one expecting to receive a lover, which, may I remind you, I am not."

Lady Darrow stifled the urge to throw a statuette at his head and instead made a motion to rise.

"Oh, how can you be so cruel, Edward! I should not be receiving anyone at all with this miserable headache! It is only because I needed to unburden myself that I forced myself to rise from my bed to receive you at all! And the only reward for my pain and efforts is an insinuating comment that can only be described as ridiculous and insulting!"

Here she seemed likely to burst into tears but put on a brave face and lifted herself from the divan. Her pink gauze robe swirled around her, gaping open at the hem to expose a pair of delicately shaped calves. The garment was wrapped loosely about her torso in a way that seemed likely to weather only the slightest movement by the wearer. Its neckline exposed rather much of the delicate roundness of her full breasts.

Confronted with the approach of such a vision, Edward steeled himself. Although he was not interested in renewing his intimate acquaintance with the lady, he nevertheless was not so immune to her charms that he did not know a moment of contemplation of the immediate pleasures such a step would bring. But only for the moment. In truth, Catharine was so far from the tantalizing vision that had kept him awake last night that he could not really contemplate sullying that ideal, or his hopes, by such disastrous action.

It was only his measure of sympathy for the forlorn emptiness he saw in her eyes—and the acknowledgment that he had once believed he loved her—that allowed him to remain in the room as she placed one delicate hand on his chest.

"Edward, you cannot know how I have regretted our parting," she began, her voice breathless with what might have been passion as she brought her body close to his, and somehow he found his arms around her.

She looked up, a pleading expression in her eyes.

"It was Blackwood, you know, who forced me to abandon you," she said and then, at the harshly skeptical look on his face, quickly continued: "Oh, I know that I did not present the picture of one so compelled when you found us that time. Nor can I claim to be insensible of my actions. But I was desperate for security and did not know how to follow the inclinations of my heart. I fell under Blackwood's spell, and somehow I could not deny him. I cannot blame you, of course, for refusing to accept such an arrangement. But I have had ample years to regret my actions, for truly the time with you was the happiest of my life."

Her voice broke on that statement, and Edward studied the luminous face that was turned up toward his. His treacherous body was betraying him as he felt her softness press against him. The full lips that trembled so slightly drew him, inexplicably, and he pressed his mouth down to them. They yielded instantly, and he explored their softness for a moment before the pressure began to increase and Lady Darrow returned the kiss with hard passion.

But his mind chose that moment to conjure the image of another woman, whose mesmerizing hazel eyes had met his across the breakfast table this morning. Those eyes held all the promise of awakening passion that any man could want, although they clearly had no inkling of the invitation that shone from them.

The lips that he now kissed, the body that his hands now caressed—these were not the ones he yearned for. And so, with a bemused look of regret, Edward gently extricated himself from Lady Darrow's arms.

In that moment, she knew the truth.

She would have told him if he had surrendered. She would have been all generosity and warned him about Blackwood's plans for his little friend. It suited her to rid herself of Blackwood, and such a disclosure would have accomplished that task quite successfully.

But, seeing her dreams die in the face of his rejection, she could not muster the altruism. The tiny little corner of her heart that held a quantity of love for him was not, it seemed,

sufficient to allow her to act to protect his heart's desire. She
had seen something more in his eyes than rejection, and she
knew now that that indeed was the appellation that could be
applied to Samantha Compton. Therefore, if Landsdown
was not to be hers, she would enjoy the small satisfaction of
preventing that upstart country miss from having him. Once
Blackwood got his hands on her, Samantha Compton would
not be fit for anyone, much less the fastidious and particular
Lord Landsdown.

"This will not do, Catharine," he said gently. "I see that
our past must remain past after all. I am sorry for your
distress, and I mean you no ill, but you must know, my dear,
that this is the end of it. I must go."

She studied his face, her own brave and sorrowful.

"Yes, Edward, I can see that you must," she said, her
eyes shimmering as she extended a long, graceful arm
toward the door.

"I am afraid that Lady Cecelia is not at home," Petersham informed Lord Formsby. "She is making calls with
her ladyship."

"And Miss Compton?" Formsby inquired politely, though
that young lady was not, in fact, the object of his call.

Here the august butler's face evinced just a trace of
concerned disapproval.

"Miss Compton has gone driving with Lord Blackwood,
my lord," Petersham said censoriously, adding after a
barely perceptible pause, "some time ago, in a closed
carriage."

Formsby's brows rose in surprise.

"Wouldn't think Lord Landsdown would go for such an
arrangement," he said.

"His lordship," Petersham intoned with what might have
been a sigh, "has been from home for most of the afternoon.
He did not inform me as to his direction, nor his plans for
returning."

Formsby caught his drift.

"Did you see, Petersham, in what direction Miss Compton and Lord Blackwood were headed?"

"No, my lord, but I believe there was some talk of avoiding habitual routes, by which I took to mean the park."

"I see. Thank you, Petersham."

Lord Formsby returned to his phaeton, knowing he must go after them but not at all certain he wished to confront Blackwood. Nevertheless, there remained the fact that Blackwood was no gentleman, and Formsby could not like the circumstance into which Miss Compton had placed herself. As Edward's friend, then, he supposed it was his duty to find them. He was at a loss, however, where to look. Blackwood must, at least, make a pretense of seeking out the park. He would not be surprised, however, if the blackguard merely kept on going far beyond that safe perimeter. Then Formsby had a brilliant inspiration. He marched back to the door where Petersham yet remained.

"If Lord Landsdown returns, Petersham, tell him I have an urge to see the gravel pits," he directed.

"Very good, sir," was the impassive response.

Samantha looked over at Lord Blackwood, who was sitting rather close by her side as the carriage rumbled down Oxbridge. She had babbled nervously during the whole of this drive and cursed her loose tongue for having suggested the pits as an alternative to the prominent aspects of the park. As a result, she was now rolling through the outskirts of Kensington, unchaperoned, with a man all of London knew was no gentleman. Edward would, of course, be apoplectic. And Samantha knew she had nothing to blame but her defiant temper. She had let Blackwood talk away her scruples and goad her into driving out with him, when every sense told her it was most improper. So far, however, Blackwood had evinced no improper behavior, so perhaps she might slip through this afternoon without incident.

The carriage slowed, and Blackwood gestured out the window.

"Nothing but piles of gravel, my dear, as you can see, but as long as we are here, you might as well look your fill."

Samantha peered out the window and saw a great quarry from which piles of stone rose here and there. There were some shacklike buildings to one side of the pits, evidently for the workers, but there was no one now in evidence. In fact, there was little sign of all of civilization. All in all, it was a thoroughly desolate place. She wished mightily that she had never thought this would be any sort of adventure.

Nevertheless, she made a show of interest, and they left the carriage, ostensibly to get a closer look.

Blackwood was standing unnecessarily close behind her. And while on previous occasions in his company, Samantha had found herself thrilled by that closeness, at this moment, she felt little else but alarm. Blackwood, in fact, now seemed less of the romantic renegade who have captured her imagination and more like a menacing, dissipated roué.

Samantha was determined, however, not to evince fear.

"I can see, my lord, that those who have disparaged this place had more sense than I. I begin to see that the idea of it was much more compelling than the reality. In truth, it seems to be just a great hole in the earth," she said. "I believe I am tired of this adventure. It would please me to return to Landsdown House."

Blackwood smiled, not altogether pleasantly, as he studied her.

"But it would not please me, my dear, for I am thoroughly enjoying your companionship," he said, his smile exposing his teeth in a manner Samantha thought reminiscent of a wolf with his prey.

"You are most flattering, Lord Blackwood. Nevertheless, I must insist on being conveyed back to Lady Landsdown's house," Samantha said in a firm tone that she hoped belied the small surge of fear that was beginning to grow stronger.

But Blackwood gave no indication that he had heard her. Instead, moving closer, he placed his arms around her waist and drew her into his embrace.

Samantha saw that he meant to kiss her, and she decided not to resist, figuring that a struggle would further inflame him. His kiss was rather moist and unpleasant, an assault upon her lips that felt as if her teeth were being pressed to the back of her throat. When his tongue began to intrude into her mouth, she wrenched her head back and looked up into his eyes with a frosty expression.

"May we return now, my lord? I find I am no longer interested in anything this place has to offer," she said coldly. "And I am persuaded that you must be as bored as I."

Blackwood's eyes blinked in surprise, and then they narrowed to a hard expression.

"You are most original, Miss Compton, but I think you must watch that sharp tongue of yours. You are wading into deep waters, and while I am prepared to tolerate a woman of spirit, I do not like to be the object of such sport."

Samantha gave an exaggerated sigh.

"And I am persuaded, Lord Blackwood, that it is not in the least necessary for you to tolerate me. Therefore, let me reiterate my request: I should like to return to Landsdown House at once," she said, and her voice held an edge of anger.

Blackwood grabbed her arms and viciously pulled her toward him. Samantha fought back a wince of pain, for she was determined to give him no evidence that she was afraid.

"I see I have failed to make myself clear, Miss Compton. I do intend that we deal together, and quite well at that," he said, giving her arm a hard squeeze.

Suddenly he released her, and her foot stumbled. He reached out to steady her, and this time the look on his face was all concern.

"There, there, Miss Compton," he said smoothly, his tone mollifying. "I have long thought you above all the fribbles and foibles and silly masquerades enacted by those we call the *ton*. I do not think you would be happy mired in such a milieu, if truth be told. I am persuaded that your spirit would chafe at society's restrictions, as mine has often done. Therefore, I do not think I am wrong in suggesting that we may be kindred spirits who could benefit and enjoy each other's company in a way that would be much more pleasing than subscribing to the *ton*'s notion of propriety."

Samantha stared at him, confused.

"I do not understand what precisely you are suggesting,

Lord Blackwood, and moreover, I do not believe I wish to. I think you best had take me home at once!''

Blackwood's laugh held real mirth.

''You poor child! You still do not understand,'' he said, his smile broad and unpleasant. ''It is my intention that you shall not have to worry about Landsdown House or its ilk. I can offer you much more than some stuffy earl! Come along, let us leave this barren place, by all means, but Landsdown House will not be our destination!''

Samantha's eyes widened in horror as Blackwood spoke, and he put his hand under her elbow to lead her back to his carriage.

''Do not be alarmed, Miss Compton. We are but going to a hunting box I own not so many miles from here. By the time this day is finished, you will care not a whit for London company!''

But Samantha turned abruptly and kicked out at him with great force. He gave a gasp of pain as her foot found its mark and doubled over as she ran with all the speed she could muster in the direction of the roadway.

''Help!'' she shouted at the coachman, who stood at his post with the horses. But he merely looked blandly in her direction. In frustration, she ran into the road.

''Won't get far, missy,'' came the coachman's laconic drawl. ''Might as well save them pretty slippers.''

But Samantha ignored him and, trying not to trip on her skirts, continued to run blindly. She did not even hear the shout that preceded the screeching wheels and the thundering hooves that stopped just inches in front of her. Suddenly she found herself face to face with two matched grays, who were breathing hard.

''How's this?'' a familiar male voice shouted.

In a daze, Samantha looked in the direction of the voice. She blinked in recognition.

''Good afternoon, Lord Formsby,'' she said politely, and then collapsed into the dirt and stone.

''Should've gone after him,'' Formsby was saying as Samantha rode beside him on the perch of his rig. ''Would have, if there wasn't the need to get you back. Call a man out for trying to abduct a female, you know. Wait until Edward hears of this!''

Samantha looked at him in alarm.

''Oh no, my lord! You cannot tell him! After all, there was no harm done. I do not believe Lord Blackwood intended to abduct me at all. Doubtless, my imagination led me to read much into a harmless outing,'' she said, hoping she sounded convincing.

He shot her a dubious look.

''Much as I'd like to oblige you, Miss Compton, this is a serious matter. You're under Edward's roof, after all.''

Samantha bit her lip. A chill drizzle had begun, adding to the gloom that now rode with them. She knew she had been foolish in going with Blackwood, and she was not eager to have Edward hear of it. But it was much worse, she realized. Her judgment had been obscured, not by the desire for Blackwood's company, but by the anger she felt toward Edward. She had wanted to defy him. Jostling along the turnpike with Lord Formsby, she realized her anger had little to do with chafing at his notions of propriety and everything to do with his visit to Lady Darrow's that afternoon.

With that knowledge, Samantha could not possibly explain to Edward why she had gone with Blackwood. He would think her a hopeless hoyden, or worse, that she had a *tendre* for Blackwood. At least the scales had finally fallen from her eyes on that score, she thought.

If only Lord Formsby could be persuaded to secrecy, but as she looked across at his set expression, she did not think the amiable lord would be so obliging.

A horseman was coming toward them, Samantha noticed idly. Then she sat up straight in alarm as the rider got closer. Edward!

Formsby had seen him, too, and reined in his team. Edward favored them both with a cold look, his back rigid in the saddle.

''As you both look drenched to the skin, I will not delay your journey home—at least I presume it is to Landsdown

House that you are bound,'' he said harshly. ''But I must say that you both have disappointed me severely.''

Formsby and Samantha heard his words in surprise, too stunned to speak. As Edward made move to leave, Formsby finally opened his mouth ''See here, Edward! 'Tis not at all what you think! Miss Compton—'' He felt a sharp nudge in his ribs from his companion. ''That is, Miss Compton . . . and I have been to the gravel pits.''

''Precisely,'' came the reply. ''Unchaperoned, in inclement weather, in an unacceptable part of town, and completely divorced from any civilized company that could impart to such a journey the tinge of respectability.''

Formsby was speechless. Outraged, Samantha forgot her fears and looked daggers at the figure on horseback.

''How like you, Edward, to jump to your own worst conclusions about everyone! It is too bad you have such a low opinion of those you call friends,'' she cried angrily.

Edward's features bore the look of one whose every emotion was under the tightest control, but he merely looked from Samantha to Formsby and then back to the road.

''As to the matter of friendship, I confess to some surprise at Lord Formsby's disappointing conduct.'' His eyes glanced back at the white-faced Henry. ''But as for you, Sam,'' he continued, ''my only surprise is that I even entertained the notion that you could behave in any other fashion. It will be a pleasure when you are no longer my responsibility.''

With that he turned his mount around, leaving them to follow him back to town.

Chapter 13

Edward glumly pondered the note in his hand informing him that Lord Cavendish would be pleased to have the earl of Landsdown and Miss Samantha Compton view the Elgin Marbles. The courtyard at Burlington House was not the most pleasant of places to spend an afternoon, now that renovations were in progress, the missive added. Nevertheless, if it pleased his lordship, Lord Cavendish would instruct his steward to make himself available to them Friday afternoon, as the workmen would be gone by then.

He threw the note on his desk in frustration. Things were getting deuced awkward with Samantha these days, and the disastrous trip to the gravel pits had only made matters worse.

Samantha had dutifully appeared in his study when summoned for an accounting of her behavior, but she had provided little in the way of an explanation. She had acquiesced meekly and uncharacteristically when he pointed out the ill-advised nature of her activities and promised never again to undertake such a foolish adventure. In that he was certain she was sincere. When he pressed her for more precise illumination of the circumstances surrounding that outing, however, she had become vague and, he thought, deliberately obfuscatory. Finally he threw up his hands in disgust and sent her on her way. They had both found the entire episode so awkward that their relations had not yet returned to what passed for normalcy these days.

As for Henry, that gentleman had become suddenly uncommunicative, although he did seek Edward out to apologize, during a rather stilted and formal conversation, for any of his actions that might have given offense. Edward formed the distinct impression that Henry himself was deeply offended at the earl's reading of his behavior. In response to Edward's inquiry, Henry insisted rather heatedly that he had no dishonorable intentions toward Miss Compton. By that statement, Edward inferred morosely, he might soon expect a declaration of honorable intentions in the form of an outright offer for Samantha's hand.

That thought was to blame for the gloomy state in which his lordship now found himself. Clearly, his own plan had not met with any degree of success. Although it had seemed, upon occasion, that Samantha had been affected by his strategy—perhaps even so far as to begin to reevaluate her feelings toward him and occasionally to think of him in terms he had hoped for—upon reflection, the matter really had progressed very little. Indeed, it seemed that his first suspicions about Henry's interest in Sam had been more than validated. If he did not do something soon, he would find himself in the unpleasant position of giving away his intended bride to his best friend. That thought was utterly untenable, but Edward was for the moment at a loss how to prevent it.

Since the gravel pits episode, moreover, Edward had noticed that Sam and Henry had been at great pains to throw off any suspicions about how matters stood between them. In fact, Henry had taken to calling on Cecelia, a move Edward supposed derived from a clever effort to deflect his own vigilance away from Sam. That Sam seemed not to be bothered by Henry's attentions to Cecelia merely confirmed in the earl's mind that she was a party to the ploy. Meanwhile, Sam had apparently undertaken to encourage every swain who ventured to send flowers around to

Landsdown House, and she did not lack for partners or suitors.

The matter was indeed becoming grave, Edward concluded, as he took up his quill to pen a reply to Lord Cavendish.

Samantha paced her room in agitation. Her manuscript lay waiting on her writing table, but she knew it would likely remain in its present unfinished state for some time. She had not been able to write anything of significance since the episode with Blackwood. Lord Deverill suddenly had become repulsive to Juliana, who sought refuge from his unwelcome attentions in the comfortable presence of her old friend, the earl of Edgedown. Their outings were never very exciting, except for the time the earl had saved Juliana from the hound, but they provided her heroine a measure of untroubled camaraderie that was vastly easier than the unpleasant fireworks that occurred in the Devil Lord's presence.

She had not confessed to Edward what had transpired that afternoon at the hands of Blackwood, and she was thankful, though somewhat surprised, that Lord Formsby had not seen fit to divulge her secret either. For Lord Formsby's sake, she would have liked to have cleared up Edward's misimpression that his friend had been responsible for such an improper situation as that in which they had found themselves. But she found she could not. It was too embarrassing to reveal the extent that Blackwood had duped her. Moreover, she knew she could never admit to him the real reason she had gone with him—her anger at Edward's visit to his ladylove. She had no right to be angry, of course. His life, after all, was his own.

Samantha shook her head. Her feelings toward Edward seemed to be wandering in strange and improper directions of late. Something had to be done. But though she had renewed her efforts at finding a suitable husband, she had found no joy in it. Mr. Worthington was nice enough, but he fawned over her like some too eager puppy. She could not imagine marriage to someone she felt like mothering. Lord

Fitzwilliam had flattered her with his attentions, but she was too conscious that he was Edward's friend. Indeed, they seemed to spend many of their conversations talking about Edward. There were several other suitors, but she found herself comparing all of them to Edward. Invariably, they were found to be wanting.

She sighed and began to wish the earl of Landsdown at the devil.

Lady Landsdown frowned at the knot that had suddenly appeared in the length of thread with which she was embroidering a piece of linen. She and the girls had been receiving calls, and Samantha had excused herself to prepare for an outing with Edward to view those musty marbles. How those two would manage to spend ten minutes in each other's company this afternoon without coming to blows would be interesting to discover.

She looked over at Cecelia, who was chatting happily with Lord Formsby. Something was afoot there, she thought, and smiled. Formsby was a delightful young man and alone among Cecelia's admirers in his apparent ability to resist her charms. Lady Landsdown decided that he was the perfect foil to her daughter, whose unrivaled beauty had naturally led her to assume that all young men would fall over themselves for a glance from such a goddess. Not that Cecelia was utterly self-centered. Indeed, she had a pleasant and intelligent nature, one that would meld quite happily with his, if matters reached that point. Intercepting Formsby's surreptitious glance at her daughter, Lady Landsdown wondered if that young man was not himself playing a deep game. She shook her head. Life was too short for such maneuverings. Why they did not get on with it was a mystery, but then there were quite a few mysteries in this house these days.

Having managed, finally, to untangle the knot, Lady Landsdown returned her thoughts to the matter of Samantha and Edward. In recent days, they had seemed barely on speaking terms. She knew that both were upset about Samantha's ill-advised and highly improper outing with

Lord Formsby, although Lady Landsdown had discounted Edward's suspicions about a match in that quarter. Indeed, it was her son who concerned her. Edward had seemed uncharacteristically unsure of himself these days, especially in Samantha's presence, and a curious suspicion of her own was beginning to dawn in Lady Landsdown's mind.

He was sitting on an upholstered leather chair waiting for Samantha, his impeccable Landsdown frame perfectly displayed this afternoon. His claret superfine coat was cut to the line, and it topped a superbly fitting pair of tan kerseymere trousers that were at the leading edge of fashion. In fact, the style had been recently adopted by the Prince Regent, to rather unfortunate effect in one of his imposing girth. Edward's snowy white muslin cravat was elegant in the extreme, despite the fact that it did not rise so high as to prevent effective movement of the head. In short, Lord Landsdown was this afternoon the epitome of effortless poise and stylish address—to all but his mother, perhaps, who did not miss the nervous twitch of his eye, the tightening of his mouth, and the hands that were held perhaps too rigidly in his lap. At Samantha's appearance on the threshold, he rose a bit too rapidly and escorted her out the door.

Lady Landsdown's brows rose slightly, but she returned to her embroidery. This Season was becoming very interesting indeed.

"I do not understand, precisely, why the marbles are at Lord Cavendish's house. Surely Lord Elgin would wish to keep them with him," Samantha said in an effort to dispel the tension in the carriage as it rumbled up Piccadilly to Burlington House.

"And so he did," Edward responded in a somewhat agreeable tone. "They reposed for years in a shed behind his house in Park Lane, but his finances finally forced him to sell the property. The Duke of Devonshire, who then owned Burlington House, offered to store them, but he had the misfortune of expiring."

"Oh, dear," murmured Samantha, her interest caught. "Whatever did Lord Elgin do?"

"The new duke was amenable to storing the marbles, but he sold the house to Cavendish, whose present renovations are causing Elgin no small anxiety. But it appears that Parliament soon will act to take them off his hands, so perhaps all the turmoil will resolve itself."

Samantha pondered the tale.

"It seems the marbles have caused Lord Elgin a good deal of trouble," she said.

"To be sure. They have cost him a fortune, made him the subject of ridicule at the clever pens of men such as Byron, and cost him his wife," Edward replied, adding as an afterthought, "although perhaps the latter loss was not so great."

She looked at him in surprise. "Why not?"

"A scandal too sordid for your ears, my dear. Suffice it to say that Lady Elgin found something more interesting than marbles with which to occupy herself. Their divorce trial, I understand, made fascinating reading in the scandal sheets."

Samantha blushed, but there was no opportunity for further conversation as their carriage pulled up to Burlington House. They were met by Lord Cavendish's steward, a young man who showed them into the courtyard, apologizing at length for the construction dust and supplies that lay everywhere.

"Unfortunately the building operations have made it necessary to move the marbles from place to place within the courtyard to give the workmen room," he was saying as he led them through the damp yard to the sculptures, most of them covered with cloths. No particular attention had been given to arranging them for display, and they lay rather haphazardly about.

Samantha stepped carefully around the statues and waited for Mr. Hammond—for that was the young man's name—to continue.

"As I said, I must apologize for their dilapidated situation, although I understand they are in excellent condition, with the exception of a few smaller pieces that were stolen during the house's extended period of vacancy," he explained. "However, I believe Lord Elgin is preparing a catalogue, which should prove helpful."

He led them to an area where some of the larger sculptures reposed near a brick wall in the courtyard. One frieze rested precariously on eight or ten bricks that had been stacked at its four corners and looked, to Samantha's eyes, as if they would fall at any moment.

Mr. Hammond removed a covering, and Samantha found herself gazing at a reclining male figure in a state of complete undress. She blushed furiously, and Mr. Hammond, following her eyes, did also.

"I beg your pardon, miss, I was looking for the charioteers, which I believe are a bit more suitable for a lady's eyes," he said, quickly moving to cover the offending specimen.

"But wait, Mr. Hammond! I have come here to see the sculptures and see them I shall," she said with determination as Edward shot her an amused glance. "Pray, who was that . . . gentleman you just showed us?"

"I cannot pretend to be very knowledgeable about the marbles, miss, but I believe that is generally considered to be either Dionysus or Heracles," he replied. "Next to him, in the same, ah . . . state, you will find one of the river gods."

Mr. Hammond stepped over some stones piled near a wall and lifted a cloth that covered a large adjacent stone.

"Now this is a four-horse chariot with soldier and charioteer," he said, gesturing. "And over there, I believe, there is a heifer being led to sacrifice."

He watched politely as Edward and Samantha stepped to the marbles he had indicated, and then cleared his throat. "You are welcome to stay as long as you like, my lord, but perhaps you will excuse me? I have some pressing duties to attend to for his lordship. I only ask that you replace the coverings when you have finished."

"You can be sure we will leave the stones as we found them," Edward said, looking pointedly at the chaos.

Their eyes followed the young man until he disappeared into the house. Then, somewhat self-consciously, they returned to the figures. Samantha saw that directly in front of them were two female figures, one of them in a reclining position. They were wearing robes whose graceful folds clearly outlined their rather generous figures.

Edward seemed to read her thoughts.

"They are very graceful, are they not?" he said, running a fingertip along one sculpted lady's bare shoulder.

Samantha watched, mesmerized, as his finger trailed down the figure's arm and followed the drape of the fabric down the length of the body to a surprisingly slender ankle. She swallowed hard.

"I wonder who they are," she said and was mortified to hear that her words emerged in a tiny, breathless sound.

"'Tis the Fates," Edward replied casually, his fingers now idly rubbing the sculpture's knee. "Two of them, anyway. They look as if they have not a care in the world, wouldn't you say?"

"Indeed," Samantha said, but she found her brain was having difficulty following the conversation.

Edward moved his hand to the figure's bare shoulder.

"Observe, Sam, the artist's exceptional skill. The muscle is perfectly placed," he said, his voice full of admiration. "You can see how it is strained in the precise position it would be if a live woman were supporting herself on her elbow in the prone manner of this lady."

He regarded the figure respectfully.

Samantha forced herself to study the shoulder, which she had to agree demonstrated the sculptor's superb knowledge of the female form. She preferred not to think, however, about the manner in which Edward had similarly acquired such knowledge. Her eyes roved from the shoulder down to the right breast, which was barely covered by the figure's gown. She took a deep breath.

"It is amazing, is it not, Edward, how accurately the human body is captured in stone?" she said finally. "It is as if these figures are but frozen in the midst of their activity."

She stopped abruptly, hoping he could not follow her

thoughts as to just *what* activity these scantily clad ladies had been contemplating.

Edward came to stand rather closely by her side and placed a hand lightly on her shoulder.

"You have said it aright, Sam, and that, of course, is the genius of it all. You see how every form is altered by action or repose," he said warmly. "The front is as different in its way as the back, with every muscle pulled and pushed into the natural position it should take for the movement illustrated."

Samantha ventured a sidelong glance at his face, which wore an enthralled look as he continued.

"It is clear that the ancients in their best and finest time understood not only the principles of anatomy, but so used them as to combine nature and idea to a form of high art," he said.

Then he turned to her, his expression thoughtful.

"It is debatable, perhaps, whether we shall ever see their equal," he said. "And although I should not like to condone the theft of the Greeks' heritage, I own to being thankful for the rare opportunity to view such extraordinary beauty."

Samantha found that she was much moved by this statement, and she stood for some moments in reflection. Here was a side of Edward she had not seen before. Strange how they had known each other for ages, yet somehow not discussed matters such as this. Nor, she realized, did she have much insight into what really moved Edward. Could it be that they did not know each other so well after all?

They spent the remainder of the afternoon in happy contemplation of the famous marbles.

"Thank you, Edward, for showing them to me," Samantha said as they left, placing her hand on his arm.

He smiled down into the face that was looking at him in friendly affection for the first time in days.

"My pleasure, Sam," he said, "although I suppose it is probably highly improper to bring a young lady to view so many incompletely attired human forms." Then he added doubtfully: "You were not offended, were you?"

She smiled and realized that her embarrassment had long

since vanished, along with the tension that had permeated the atmosphere earlier.

"I suppose I should own to being scandalized into a case of the vapors, Edward," she said, her eyes dancing. "But truly, it was the most enjoyable afternoon I have spent in years."

He extended his arm, and she linked hers through it as they walked back to the carriage in perfect harmony.

In an odd manner, not precisely clear to either of the parties, the viewing of the marbles served to return a measure of harmony to Landsdown House. That is, until the offers of marriage started arriving for Samantha.

Chapter 14

The first to present himself in Edward's study was Mr. Daniel Worthington, to no one's surprise. That young man had dressed for the occasion as if he were preparing to meet a member of the royal family, his peacock blue coat apparently just having left the needle of one of Bond Street's most noted pretenders, his waistcoat fashioned in a brilliant shade of parrot green woven with a thread of mustard yellow. No fault could be found with his boots; Edward could discern the work of Hoby there and thought perhaps there was hope for the lad yet. But the entire ensemble hung on its wearer rather loosely, as if waiting for him to fill it out, perhaps in another year or so.

Edward pondered the young gentleman who, mumbling in an embarrassed but most determined manner, presented his qualifications for the inestimable Miss Compton's hand. Edward had already ascertained Mr. Worthington's acceptability by virtue of a connection with Lord Wexford that meant a sizable income and eventually even a title. But Edward had no illusions that Samantha would accept this young man. Accordingly, he had not the slightest hesitation in informing Mr. Worthington that his suit must certainly be considered a highly eligible one and that he was welcome to present his case to Miss Compton herself.

"I gather you have not yet spoken to her?" Edward asked gently.

Mr. Worthington looked down at his feet for a moment and then raised his eyes hopefully.

"No, sir. I thought to apply to you first. I know you are not her guardian precisely, but as you stand as her sponsor and friend, I thought it only proper," came the response.

"My mother and the late earl were Miss Compton's godparents," Edward said. "Her mother is an invalid, moreover, so you acted quite correctly in assuming that I have the responsibility of seeing to the settling of her future. But I should warn you that Miss Compton speaks her own mind and makes her own decisions. You must apply to her directly."

Mr. Worthington made a slight adjustment to his cravat, which was starched to a fare-thee-well and rose to a point just below his earlobe, so that it was very difficult for his head to move freely. He cleared his throat.

"I suppose it is presumptuous of me to think that such a lady of Miss Compton's stature and beauty would even consider my offer, but I have thought it over for many weeks and . . . well, my lord, I *must* speak!"

That remark had been delivered with such fervor that Edward feared for Mr. Worthington's nerves and quickly offered him a glass of Madeira. After disposing of it in a single gulp, Mr. Worthington quit the room in search of Samantha, although Edward thought he looked nervous enough to be headed to the gallows.

Now that the Season was winding down, a parade of gentlemen succeeded Mr. Worthington into Edward's study, all of them variations on that first deeply enthralled caller. There was Mr. Bruce, who could claim twenty thousand pounds a year; Mr. Bloodgood, who was heir to a viscountcy; and Lord Kingsley, who needed to marry an heiress because his estates were to let but whose infatuation apparently blinded him to Samantha's poverty. There was even a call from the widowed Lord Dalymore, his brain nearly addled by spirits but drawn by Miss Compton's youthful energy to consider her the perfect mama for his brood of eleven.

Each of these gentlemen subsequently were gently turned away by the object of their affections—at least Edward presumed that was the case, since Sam did not come to him with any news about impending nuptials. Although he burned with curiosity to know how she had received these suitors, he did not press her, nor, in fact, did they discuss it at all.

Edward bore this procession of hopefuls with a sanguine-ness that rose from the view that each of them represented a perfectly dreadful choice for Sam's husband. And although he knew she felt compelled to wed, he did not think she was desperate enough to choose any of these so obviously inadequate specimens. He had to consider the bothersome matter of Henry, of course, but luckily that gentleman had not yet seen fit to visit his study on that type of mission. In fact, Henry seemed curiously occupied with Cecelia these days.

Edward judged that as he had not yet come up with a plan to make Sam see himself as the answer to her prayers, he would in the interim simply enjoy their newfound harmony. They had taken to strolling in the park of an afternoon, playing chess when it was too rainy to go out, and whiling away the occasional evening at home with a hand or two of whist or easy discourse about the day's events.

It was a comfortable life, reminiscent of their former relationship, although there was in fact a subtle difference. It was understood, somehow, that this harmony did not allow for the intrusion of those unsettling and altogether uncomfortable sensations that both of them had noted in previous weeks in the presence of the other. Edward had left off trying to awaken Samantha to those passions; instead, he was content for the nonce to reestablish some measure of compatibility that they had lost. He knew that both of them, on some level of their awareness, groped for an understanding of these feelings, nay, perhaps even wished that they might be fully explored. But he knew also that both had decided for now to sacrifice them for a friendship they

valued; accordingly, they had consigned any other feelings
to an inner chamber of their brains which would not, could
not, be disturbed.

Edward accepted this situation as merely temporary until
he could ascertain what next must be done, for he still
determined to win Samantha. And so, while her plethora of
suitors shook his complacency somewhat, their patent
unsuitability allowed him to ease his mind and bide his time.

But, in the waning weeks of the Season, there appeared in
his study Lord Brendan Fitzwilliam, whose presence in that
context shook him to the core. Unlike the others, Fitz had
already spoken to Samantha.

Samantha vastly enjoyed Lord Fitzwilliam's company. In
fact, she found that her eyes often searched for him
immediately when they arrived at one function or another.
He was older than many of the other gentlemen of her
acquaintance, of an age with Edward, to be precise. Like
Edward, he had about him a maturity of manner and an
elegance of conversation that made him a most enjoyable
and witty companion.

Further, Lord Fitzwilliam was a most attractive gentleman. He was tall, nearly as tall as Edward, although broader
of shoulder and something of a Corinthian. There was a
dimple in his left cheek that, when his lordship found something particularly amusing, suddenly appeared to charming
effect. If his reputation was to be believed, he vastly
enjoyed the ladies of all stripes who pursued him. But he
had never inclined himself to the parson's mousetrap, and
Samantha welcomed the opportunity to appreciate a gentleman's companionship without concerning herself with his
matrimonial inclinations.

Therefore, as they waltzed at Lady Forthman's town
house one evening, Samantha was surprised to feel Lord
Fitzwilliam's arm press her close. That was followed by an
urgent request, delivered in tantalizingly low tones, for a
private stroll in their hostess's gardens. Samantha felt a
surge of alarm, but quickly acquiesced.

"My dear Samantha," he began when they had gained

the garden. Then he added with a twinkle in his eye, "You do not mind if I call you my 'dear Samantha'? I must confess it is a liberty I would be loath to abandon."

Samantha beheld his fascinating dimple and smiled her assent. "I do not see how I can force you to take back your words, my lord!"

He laughed gently and caught her hand, using it to pull her closer to him.

"I will not stand on ceremony, Samantha, nor offer you pretty phrases that I am certain you have heard to fulsome excess from the many suitors who have offered you their names," he said, and saw confirmation in her answering blush.

He took her chin in his, and Samantha was surprised that those large hands were capable of such a gentle caress.

"I can only hope you are not considering any of them, Samantha," he said, his face suddenly serious, "for I would like very much to marry you."

Samantha gave a sudden intake of breath and averted her eyes. He immediately released her.

"I did not do that prettily, I know, and perhaps you would rather it done so," he said with chagrin. "I can only plead my lack of expertise in this area. You are the only woman to whom I have made such an offer."

Abruptly he went down on one knee. His massive hands held hers.

"Very well, then, my dear Miss Compton," he said. "I find that I can no longer live in a world in which I do not have the privilege of seeing your beautiful eyes across the breakfast table each morning, eyes that hold the sun and the moon and the stars. . . ."

"Stop!" Samantha said, laughing. "Pray, do not continue in this manner, Lord Fitzwilliam! And pray, do get up! You are embarrassing me beyond all thought! I do not care for such pretty phrases. In truth, I am mightily sick of them, as you quite accurately guessed!"

They both laughed in earnest as Lord Fitzwilliam rose, and anyone who had stumbled upon them then would not have been faulted for thinking that they shared some wonderful joke. As indeed perhaps they did.

Suddenly Samantha noticed that Lord Fitzwilliam was no longer laughing, but was staring at her in a disconcerting manner. Slowly he took her face in his hands and bent down to her. His kiss was gentle, a relaxed, reassuring caress that, hesitantly, she returned. She felt the pressure increase, but she was not moved to resist it. Finally Lord Fitzwilliam raised his head.

"I think we should deal quite well together, Samantha," he said, his green eyes sparkling. "I would not try to curb your independence, nor stifle that frank tongue of yours. I have a comfortable fortune, and we might live wherever you choose. Ours should be a boisterous, happy family, with children who owe their beauty and their spirit to their lovely, incomparable mother."

Samantha felt tears form in her eyes at his words, though she could not say why. It was all she had dreamed of, and more certainly than she had expected to find. There was no reason to hesitate, surely. An image of Edward's haunting blue eyes passed briefly before her mind's eye, but she quickly banished it. She had depended on Edward's friendship for too much. It was time to stop the disconcerting thoughts that had wandered untrammeled in her mind in recent weeks. They sought ground that would not bear fruit, she knew, perhaps because they were only the fantasies of a silly girl. Indeed, she had welcomed the return to a measure of their easy friendship and the lessening of tensions between them; that the recent tranquility was less satisfying than it had been in the past did not bear exploring.

No, it was time to put her childhood behind her. Edward would never think of her as anything but a sister or family friend. And while she did not love Lord Fitzwilliam, that had never been a requirement of marriage for her. A dream, perhaps, but not a necessity. She must marry, and none of the gentlemen who had offered her that state had led her to envision anything other than abject boredom for the rest of her days. Lord Fitzwilliam, at least, would be an amiable and enjoyable companion.

He was looking at her with a question in eyes.

"I should be happy to marry you, sir," Samantha replied.

Edward stared at the man who had just shattered his peaceful complacence.

"Samantha has agreed to this?" he asked in a strangled voice, his heart demanding the denial that his brain knew would not come.

"Yes. I thought I mentioned that she had accepted me last night," Lord Fitzwilliam replied, perplexed. "I do believe you are not attending, Edward. Or is it—" Lord Fitzwilliam broke off. "Do you not approve, my friend? I realize my past history does not precisely commend me as ideal husband material. But you need have no worries on that score. I fully expect to be a faithful and amiable husband to Samantha."

Edward rose then and spent a silent minute pouring two glasses of brandy, spilling several drops with unaccustomed awkwardness.

"Nay, Fitz, for I believe that you would treat her well—I should say that if you did not, you must needs answer to me—but I wonder . . . that is, do you love Samantha?" The earl's eyes were somber as he extended a glass to Lord Fitzwilliam.

That gentleman was somewhat taken aback.

"Love? To tell the truth, we did not speak of it," he said, bewildered. "I would be the first to admit that it would be a happy circumstance. Still, I cannot think that it is an absolute necessity at the moment."

Lord Fitzwilliam sipped his brandy and studied his friend.

"I would like to have your blessing, Edward, for we both value your friendship. What gives you pause? If you are concerned about my finances, I will instruct my man of business to provide you with a complete accounting. As for a settlement, I am aware of Samantha's situation and have no need or expectations of wealth from her. It is enough that she has agreed to marry me."

Edward swallowed the lump in his throat and raised his glass to his friend.

"You have my heartfelt felicitations, Fitz," he said.

Cecelia, however, was horrified when she heard the tidings from Samantha.

"You cannot be serious, Samantha! This is the worst news! You know that Lord Formsby believes it is Lord Fitzwilliam whom Edward is trying to force me to wed! Now he will know that it was all a hum! What shall I do?"

Samantha drew a brush through her thick hair and pondered the matter calmly.

"We shall just have to keep it secret," she said in a matter-of-fact tone. "I'll wager it can be done for a while. But, Cecelia, you really must bring Lord Formsby around. I should think that would not be too difficult for an Incomparable! By the way, do you think you might wish me happy?"

Cecelia colored guiltily and rushed to embrace her friend.

"Oh, do forgive me, Samantha! It is just . . . well, Lord Formsby is the most frustrating man! I seem to be getting nowhere!"

"Well, you shall have to get somewhere soon, Cecelia. We shall just have to put our minds to it."

After that, Lord Fitzwilliam was a steady visitor at Landsdown House, a fact that did nothing to disabuse Lord Formsby of the notion that that gentleman was intended for Cecelia. Fitzwilliam was perfectly happy to withhold any betrothal announcement, never being one to care for convention or such details that so consumed the ladies of his set.

Secrecy also suited Samantha, who felt an inexplicable reluctance to take such a public step. Neither did Lady Landsdown raise any objection. In fact, she was delighted to plan the announcement as the high point of her masquerade that would bring the Season to a close. Perhaps by that time Cecelia would have an announcement of her own. As for Edward, he had his own motives for delaying an announcement, chief among them the fervent hope that something would happen to change Samantha's mind.

Samantha did, however, write to her mother that she had been honored by a proposal of marriage from Lord Fitz-william and had indicated her acceptance. She also began to write again on her manuscript.

Lord Deverill had been dismissed as a rakehell and seducer, thoroughly unsuitable for the respectable Miss Morriston, who was betrothed at last to the most eligible and estimable Lord Neal. The earl of Edgedown, her longtime friend, was to give the bride away.

> She was walking down the aisle at St. George's on Edgedown's arm, the figure waiting at the altar a hazy vision she could not quite discern. Her mama was smiling tearfully from her pew at the front of the church, and Juliana knew she could not disappoint her, as this was their only opportunity for financial security. But this most important moment of her life had a strange, dreamlike quality that left her profoundly uneasy.
>
> The vision at the altar got closer, and still she could not quite make him out. The moment had come for Edgedown to hand her over to Lord Neal. She turned and looked up into Edgedown's face and the clear blue eyes that seemed to penetrate to her very soul. Suddenly she knew she could not go through with this marriage. He was extricating his arm from hers. She felt an inexorable sense of loss.
>
> "No!" she cried, turning back to Edgedown, whose face froze in shocked surprise. "I cannot!"

And whyever not, you milk and water miss, Samantha thought in disgust, tossing the manuscript onto the floor in her frustration. Juliana had turned out to be a most contrary heroine, rejecting the exciting if diabolical Lord Devil and now ruining the best marriage opportunity she was likely to get in a lifetime. Why?

Samantha looked at the clock on the mantel in her bedchamber. It was nearly two o'clock in the morning. She had turned to her work to ease her sleeplessness, but clearly that was no solution. Suddenly she felt trapped—by her pretty room, her fashionable dresses, her relentless obligations, and by a sense of profound dissatisfaction, for which she could not find a clear reason. She needed to talk to someone—no, not just anyone. She tossed on her wrapper and fled her chamber.

Candlelight shone from under the study door, as she had hoped. Samantha paused outside and wondered why she was there and what, if anything, she meant to tell Edward. She did not know the answer, only that she must see him. Gently she pushed on the door, and it creaked open.

Edward was sitting in a chair near his desk, a book in his hand and a glass of what might have been port or brandy at his elbow. His cravat was undone, and the top of his shirt was open at the neck. His tousled blond hair was in disarray, and he was looking at where she stood in the doorway with a strange, rather tormented expression.

"Good evening, Edward," she said hesitantly, wishing suddenly that she had not come.

"Sam."

It was his only acknowledgment.

She did not know whether to leave or stay. Finally she turned to go.

"Did you wish to speak to me?" a harsh voice said then. She turned.

"Why . . . it was just that I was having trouble sleeping and, well, I thought perhaps you were awake also," she said hesitantly.

"And why did you imagine that was the case?"

Samantha looked at the hard glint in his eye and felt a chill through her veins.

"I do not know, but it seems I was correct, after all. You do seem to be far from thinking about sleep," she said doubtfully.

"And what do you suppose I have been thinking about?" came the relentless question.

"I—I do not know, Edward, and perhaps I'd best leave. This does not seem to be a good time to talk after all," she said and stepped out the door.

A pair of arms was around her in a flash, turning her toward him and the dim light of the candle. She looked up into a face that was suddenly all concern.

"Did you need to speak to me, Sam?" he said, his tone surprisingly gentle. Compassion shone from his eyes, which radiated an odd brightness in the flickering light. "I did not mean to frighten you away."

Samantha gave a nervous laugh and was suddenly quite conscious of the arms that held her shoulders. As if reading her thoughts, he released her. He gestured to another chair and poured another glass while she sat.

"Drink this," he commanded. "If nothing else, it should eliminate your sleep problems."

The golden liquid burned her throat, and she gave a sputtering cough as it made its way down. But after a moment she felt a comforting warmth spread through her.

Edward was studying her, his face inscrutable. One hand absentmindedly stroked the rim of his glass, and Samantha was mindful of a great cat watching and waiting. Finally he spoke.

"What did you wish to talk about?" he said quietly, his eyes holding hers with a strange intensity.

She shifted in her chair. This was not the Edward she was used to. In fact, she did not seem to know him at all any longer. A sudden desolation overwhelmed her.

"I only thought . . . that is—oh, Edward! I had it all planned out, you know, and now that it has happened, it seems exceedingly distressing!" She twisted her hands in great agitation.

There was silence for a moment before he spoke.

"You are speaking in riddles, Sam. Are you referring to your impending marriage? If you are having doubts about Fitzwilliam, rest assured that your engagement can be ended in a thrice."

Samantha shook her head.

"It is not Lord Fitzwilliam, for he is everything that one can hope to find in a husband," she said, oblivious of the fleeting look of pain that met this statement. "No, it is deeper than that. It must have something to do with me—I feel somehow empty, as if everything his lordship could offer is not enough. And yet, who could have dreamed I would have been fortunate enough to secure such an offer as this? Only . . . well, is this what marriage is all about?''

''I do not know what you mean.'' His voice was flat.

She looked at him and then took a sip of her drink, perhaps for the courage it gave her, for it was beginning to loosen her tongue.

''No, of course not, for you never have even considered getting leg-shackled,'' she said. Then, remembering Lady Darrow, she hastily amended: ''Or if you have, I am sure you have not told me. Not that it is my concern, of course!''

His brows rose at that, and she looked away quickly, silently cursing her awkward tongue. But she went on.

''I never had the least illusion, Edward, that it was necessary to love one's husband at the outset. I suppose that comes in time, if at all. But my silly romantic notions seem to have distorted my reasoning. I can't help thinking that suddenly I will see that dashing fellow of my dreams. It is foolish—'fluff and nonsense,' you once called it.''

Both were silent for some minutes, remembering the conversation that seemed to have occurred a century ago.

''I repeat, Sam: it is not necessary for you to marry Fitz if you do not wish it,'' Edward said at last.

But Samantha was already beginning to feel foolish at her confession. She took a final sip and rose. Stifling a yawn, she shook her head, trying to banish the cobwebs.

''Oh, but I am such a dreamer, Edward, as you have said time and again. I shall save my dreams for my silly manuscripts. They do not belong here,'' she said and was mortified to find her voice breaking. Then, with more resolve, she added: ''I shall wed Lord Fitzwilliam and be a most proper and dutiful wife!''

Suddenly she felt the tears come, unbidden, and quickly she turned to leave. But when she would have quit the room, Edward reached out and touched her sleeve. As Samantha turned and looked into his face, her small measure of control vanished, and she burst into tears.

He gathered her into his arms while she cried long and

hard into his chest. As he patted her back and stroked her hair, he might have been thinking of the little girl he had comforted in just that manner so often before. But that child was gone forever, and the problems of the woman who had replaced her could not merely be kissed away.

At least he did not think they could.

Samantha lifted her head and wiped her red eyes, looking at him through her tears with an embarrassed smile. When she would have spoken, he placed one finger gently on her lips to silence her. Instinctively her lips parted. Her eyes grew wide as she stared, mesmerized, at his face.

"Shhh," he said, and his fingertip lingered to softly trace her mouth.

Slowly he brought his lips to hers, brushing them with excruciating gentleness before, almost regretfully, moving away.

She stared at him mutely.

"Good night, Sam," he said quietly and, turning her around, nudged her gently in the direction of the stairs.

But it was many hours before Samantha slept, for now she knew the source of her troubles, the truth about her feelings that had danced around the edges of her brain, eluding her for so many confusing weeks. And there was nothing at all to be done for it.

Chapter 15

In a moment of utter madness born of desperation, the earl of Landsdown conceived the notion of abducting Samantha. It was not the sort of thing that was in his nature, of that he was certain; nevertheless, as the idea presented itself as the only feasible way out of his despair, he wondered if, in fact, this were a long-dormant aspect of his character that had only been waiting for a moment such as this. It was not a question to which he gave undue thought, except to observe ruefully to himself that it was a course at great variance with the image he presented to the world and indeed, with his own public statements.

He recalled, and knew it for a great irony, his conversation with Samantha not too many weeks ago in which he ridiculed such a tactic employed by one of her heroes. But in fact it was that very conversation that had now given rise to the thought that an abduction might serve his purpose very well.

That Samantha Compton was an incurable romantic could not be denied. But he knew that whatever her dreams, she would not permit them to stand in the way of the practical necessity of providing for her mother and herself. She did not love Fitz, of that he was certain, although perhaps she liked that gentleman well enough. In the absence of any claim upon her heart, however, she was apparently determined to proceed with the wedding. It was Edward's desperate hope that, were she to be offered such a bold opportunity for love as he planned to place before her, she would decide otherwise.

Edward blamed himself for the fact that Sam had not yet come to realize that he was her proper life's companion. He had been too cautious, too reluctant to venture far out on this precarious limb on which he was perched. As a result, his campaign to bring her around to his view had not progressed far enough to ensure that his declaration would be received with anything but horrified disbelief. Moreover, to take such a step now that she was betrothed to someone else—and to one of his friends, at that—would be unfair and, he thought, somewhat ill mannered.

But time was running out. Sam needed to see for herself that she could not wed a man she did not love, that ending her engagement was the only proper course; he could then, with honor, offer his hand in place of poor Fitz's.

His course was clear. To wit, he must demonstrate that her dreams were attainable, that love and passion were not figments of her overactive imagination—in short, that the hero of her novels was before her very eyes.

It sounded well enough, but there were difficulties, not the least of which was his own trepidation at such a risky step. Until now, his powers of persuasion over Sam and others of her sex had been exercised in those ways that were not only familiar to him, they were so subtly applied as to allow him to pull back at any moment. The earl of Landsdown had never, since he achieved the full flower of his adulthood, allowed himself to reach the point of no return with any woman. Inaccessible to the very core, he had never truly risked his heart in the name of love. Now he found the irrevocableness of such a step both awesome and frightening. Still, for stakes such as these, he had no choice.

The other difficulties were less profound. He would have to don a disguise; it was his intention to give her some days to consider her predicament, and so the revelation of her hero's identity would be saved for his mother's masquerade—a night on which as it now stood, Sam and Fitz's betrothal was to be announced. But by then, if he managed it correctly, Sam's head would be full of her dashing highwayman.

Moreover, it was necessary to obtain the cooperation of his coachman, but fortunately that individual had been so long in his employ that he did not bat an eye at his lordship's outlandish instructions. Finally, it was necessary to remind Cecelia of her intention to visit her ailing nanny, who lived just past the outskirts of town, and to prod her with the accusing suggestion that she was so caught up in the Season that she appeared to have so forgotten the sweet woman who practically raised them. As he had expected, Cecelia was so racked with guilt that she proposed a visit the next afternoon. His proposal that Samantha accompany Cecelia was readily agreed to.

So, on an afternoon less than a week after the night Edward and Samantha had met in his study, the Landsdown carriage rumbled over the cobblestones on its way to Nanny Stedham's little cottage some few miles north of Paddington.

The visit itself was uneventful, consisting chiefly of the bestowal upon the elderly pensioner of a basket of fruit and some other provisions, and the delighted discussion between that deserving lady and Cecelia of the details of the latter's hugely successful Season. Samantha was so silent as Cecelia and Nanny Stedham chattered away that she knew her behavior bordered on rudeness. But she found she could not force herself to put aside her troubled thoughts.

On the return journey, Cecelia gave up trying to enlist Samantha in conversation, and the trip continued in a companionable, if relentless, silence. No doubt, Samantha reflected as the sun cast its waning rays on their carriage, Cecelia would have been shocked to realize that it was her own brother who dominated her thoughts.

Samantha had been profoundly affected by that brief, almost reverential kiss he had bestowed upon her, although she knew it was prompted only by compassion at her plight.

But alas, she could no longer deny the fact that she was thoroughly and hopelessly in love with Edward, and the realization gave her great pain. Even if she were not betrothed to another, Edward had never shown any inclination to confer his heart on any lady, much less the persistent little shadow from his childhood.

Yet had she only imagined the current between them in recent weeks, and the occasional look in his eye that made her skin tingle and her heart pound faster? No doubt she was spinning fantasies; nevertheless, something made her reluctant to ascribe it all to her vivid imagination.

She suppressed a bitter laugh. It really did not matter, did it? For if there *was* something there, it was not sufficient to induce Edward to speak. There had been no declaration, no words to suggest that he had any wish to alter their relationship. And since he had not spoken, she could not. She must forever keep her love a secret, continuing to play the role of congenial friend. She frowned. Was she being fair to Lord Fitzwilliam? How could she become his wife when she loved another? For that matter, could she manage to deny what was in her own heart?

"I wish we had gotten an earlier start," Cecelia was saying, "but it took John Coachman forever to bring the carriage round. And see now, the sun is nearly set. It will be dark before we get home!"

They were approaching the towing path, and the bustle of London had not yet begun to replace the verdant green of the countryside.

Suddenly, a shot rang out and a shout reverberated through the emerging twilight. The carriage came abruptly to a halt.

"Highwaymen!" Cecelia cried.

In alarm, Samantha leaned over to peer out the window of the carriage door. She saw nothing there, but in a moment the door was opened by a masked man cloaked in black.

"I'll take your fine baubles, if you please," announced a gruff voice from behind the mask.

"How dare you—!" Samantha began, but Cecelia interrupted her sharply.

"Do not argue with him, Samantha!" she said, instantly removing her rings and a necklace and handing them to the outstretched hand.

"Good advice, missy," the voice growled menacingly, and Samantha reluctantly began trying to remove the only jewelry she wore, an amethyst ring that had been a gift from her father.

It would not, however, come off.

"'Tis stuck!" she said. "You will just have to make do with what you have! I cannot think one small ring makes much of a difference at all events. It is hardly valuable!"

In response to her declaration, the highwayman simply reached further into the coach and pulled her out toward him. Cecelia shrieked in horror.

"Let me go!" Samantha commanded, but the fear in her voice gave the order a pitiful quiver.

Wordlessly the man lifted her onto his horse and swung himself up behind her. Without so much as a backward glance, he spurred his mount to a gallop.

Samantha was in a state of utter shock. It was useless to protest or even to talk, as the wind would have flung her words to the far corners, so she endured the jostling ride in stunned silence. The man's arms were firmly around her middle as he held the reins, and their position left his body pressed against her back in a most intimate manner. She supposed such embarrassment was the least of her worries at the moment, however.

After perhaps a quarter hour, they came upon a narrow dirt road and followed it through some woods to what appeared to be a small cottage, although darkness had descended in earnest, and Samantha could not discern much of her surroundings. The man carried her into the modest structure as easily as if she had been a feather. Oddly, the sensation of being in his arms was not unpleasant, and Samantha closed her eyes in mortification.

He tossed her onto a small bed and lit a smoky candle, but it cast only the barest light, bathing the room in an eerie dimness that only added to the nightmarish quality of the episode.

Samantha watched her captor's movements in silence, trying to determine who or what he might be. His voice was rough, but his arms had been surprisingly gentle. He was tall, and his form appeared lean and athletic; he had certainly managed to lift her with little effort. But she could tell little else about him. He was dressed all in black and wore a mask that covered three-fourths of his face. There were slits for his eyes, but those she could not make out in the darkness. Only his mouth was not covered. His hair appeared thick and black.

As she studied him, the man suddenly turned and advanced toward her.

"Who are you?" Samantha demanded contemptuously to cover her fear. Then a thought occurred to her, and she added: "You are not Lord Blackwood, are you?"

The figure stopped abruptly, as if confused. There was a long moment of silence, and the man's generous mouth constricted.

"Why would you think such a thing?" he asked in an indignant but demanding tone that adjured her to respond.

Samantha eyed him nervously, noticing that his gruff baritone now bore the unmistakable accent of a gentleman.

"Just that, as you . . . er, he . . . failed at the gravel pits, owing to the appearance of Lord Formsby, I . . . thought perhaps this was another such effort . . ." She broke off, suddenly frightened by the current of anger she felt emanating from him.

When she thought he would have spoken, however, he suddenly seemed to think better of it and turned away. Finally, in a constricted voice, he said, "I am not Lord Blackwood."

In the ensuing silence, Samantha pondered this statement and wondered at the depth of feeling behind it. Now that she studied him, she could see that he did not much resemble Blackwood, except for the black hair. This villain seemed somewhat younger. Could her captor be wearing a wig?

"Well, that is a relief, for I really did not like him by half, but I daresay that you are not much better," she said scornfully in a bid to distract him. "Abducting a young woman is not the act of an honorable man."

Then, in sudden inspiration, she added: "My father—we live nearby, you know—will have dispatched a dozen of his men to look for me by now. You will wish to flee immediately, I am certain."

He turned back to her then, and Samantha thought she detected the slightest crack in that stern demeanor. In fact, it appeared that a smile had begun to steal over his features. For some reason, she found that she was beginning to lose her fear.

"Ah, but I know that that is not the case, Miss Compton. You have quite an imagination."

Samantha's eyes widened. "You know my name?" she asked incredulously.

The man advanced toward the bed and sat down on it gingerly. He picked up her hand and stared into her face.

"Indeed," the gruff voice continued. "I know a great deal about you, for I have long admired you. I have been but waiting for an opportunity such as this."

With that, he pressed her hand to his lips and kissed it lingeringly. Samantha felt a sharp sensation of fear war with another that was coursing through her body.

She decided to keep him engaged in conversation.

"What, sir, are your intentions?" she demanded. "I can see that you are no gentleman!"

He smiled more broadly and moved close to whisper in her ear, his lips lightly brushing her skin as he spoke.

"I never claimed to be a gentleman, Miss Compton, only a man enraptured by a lady's charms."

Samantha felt a strong surge of anger at his brazen encroachment upon her person.

"I do not care what you are! You have abducted and assaulted me, and I demand, sirrah, to be released forthwith!"

His only answer was to take her chin forcefully between his hands. She opened her mouth to scream, and he quickly covered it with one of his hands.

"I shall not harm you, Miss Compton, I promise you that.

I only wanted you to know that you have a secret admirer who but waits for the opportunity to serve you.''

In answer, Samantha bit his hand as hard as she could. He yelped in pain and jumped back, in the process tripping over an oaken bucket that stood near the bedside. As Samantha watched in amazement, her captor tumbled over backward, landing in an undignified position in which his posterior aspect bore the brunt of his fall. Further, the man remained thus for a moment, apparently having lost his bearings.

Helpless to stop herself, Samantha burst into laughter. She knew she should have taken advantage of his disadvantageous state to flee, but somehow he did not look so threatening in such a position.

''That was well done, sir!'' she cried, nearly doubled over with laughter. ''Doubtless, no highwayman has ever entertained his captive so thoroughly. Dare I hope for a repeat performance?''

When he had risen to his feet, a task achieved with some awkwardness, Samantha saw his features lighten and knew that he, too, had seen the humor in his situation.

''I daresay, Miss Compton, that my loss of poise can be laid at your door. You are a thoroughly frustrating victim!'' he said, his mouth curving in an embarrassed smile.

Samantha regained her composure and fixed him with a questioning look. He was a most unusual villain. For a long breathtaking and silent moment they looked at each other. She could not have moved if she had wished to. Which, she found, she did not.

Finally she spoke. ''Why am I here?'' she asked softly.

There was a brief pause, and then he looked away. ''Because there was no other way to bring my existence to your attention,'' he said quietly.

She heard the sincerity in his voice and thought, moreover, that there was a sadness there also. ''But you speak like a gentleman. Why must you disguise your identity?''

''Because it is not yet time for you to know it,'' he replied evasively.

Samantha frowned in confusion. ''When will the time be right, pray tell?''

"At Lady Landsdown's masquerade."

She pondered this statement, no longer surprised that he seemed to know everything about her and her activities.

"Then you really do not intend to harm me?" she asked, regarding him steadily.

The figure advanced toward her, and, despite the darkness, Samantha detected a subtle shifting in his mood.

"No, but that is not to say that I am quite ready to set you free," he said quietly.

Now, with a little surge of fear, Samantha sensed his purpose. She jumped off the bed and ran for the door. But she managed to get only a few feet when he grabbed her from behind. They crashed to the floor as one, hitting with a thud, and Samantha felt the breath knocked out of her. She could not move, but he moved for her, gently rolling her onto her back and studying her face intently. As his body pinned hers, she found to her great dismay that it was not at all an unpleasant experience. With a great effort, she banished that treacherous thought and roused herself to struggle.

Immediately the man captured her hands and held them above her head, his body moving more thoroughly over hers to render her completely immobile. As she stared, riveted by the intensity he radiated, his mouth lowered to hers. But instead of the assault she expected, the man spoke in a gruff, barely audible whisper against her lips.

"Tell me about your dreams, Miss Compton."

Samantha was flabbergasted.

"My . . . dreams?"

"Yes. You do have them? There must be faces you see as you fall asleep at night, perhaps a gentleman or two who enlivens your nocturnal adventures."

"I beg your pardon, sir!" she said, aghast. "This is a highly improper conversation!"

"Just so," the figure said, and then his mouth did take hers.

It was a kiss unlike anything she had ever known. His lips were soft, caressing hers gently in a way that seemed familiar, yet awakened unfamiliar sensations. They brushed

back and forth in a tantalizing manner until finally the
pressure increased, and Samantha realized in amazement
that she had been wanting and waiting for that all along.

His passion found a silent answer in her own, and for a
long time their lips claimed each other as their bodies
sought closer contact. Samantha felt his hand on her breast
and knew a strange yearning for the completion of whatever
they had begun. But just as she felt herself utterly lost, the
lips became suddenly gentle, finally withdrawing altogether.

"And now that you are truly in danger, Miss Compton,"
the rough voice said harshly, "it is time to return you to
safety."

As Samantha looked at him in stunned confusion, the
highwayman suddenly swept her up into his arms and out
the door. He tossed her onto his horse and swung up behind
her without a word.

As they rode through the darkness, Samantha felt enveloped by his arms in a strange world in which there was no
sense of time or place. In her torpor, she only knew that she
wanted their rendezvous to go on and on, unfettered by the
trappings of reality.

But it did not. At the outskirts of Paddington, he quickly
hailed a hackney cab and helped her into the conveyance as
the startled driver stared at his strange appearance.

"But who are you? Where will I see you?" Samantha
managed weakly.

"The masquerade," the voice replied tersely. "I shall
wear a black domino."

Her eyes stared in dazed incomprehension, and after a
pause he added gravely: "My intentions, Miss Compton,
are entirely honorable."

With that, he shut her into the hackney, and it rolled off
in the direction of Charles Street.

The hue and cry that Cecelia had set off when the
Landsdown coach returned to London had so far resulted in
a great throng of people being assembled in the foyer of

Landsdown House, all of them shouting varying instructions to everyone and no one.

Lady Landsdown was wringing her hands and demanding that the watch be called. Lord Fitzwilliam was ready to set out on his own and barked orders for the commandeering of a swift horse from Edward's stable. Lord Formsby, who seemed solely concerned with Cecelia's part of the ordeal, had that nearly hysterical young lady in a corner questioning her intently as to whether or not she was harmed. John Coachman's baffling inability to describe the criminal sent the lot of them into a frenzy of frustration. After a quarter hour of such confusion, Lord Fitzwilliam finally shouted for silence.

"I do not care what any of you wish to do! I am leaving immediately. We have already lost valuable time, as no one even thought to summon me until nearly an hour after Cecelia arrived! As we dither, Samantha's very life may be in danger!"

"Oh, where is Edward?" Lady Landsdown cried. "I cannot think we should do anything until he can be found! I am persuaded he will know best what is to be done."

"And in the meantime, Samantha may be enduring unspeakable assaults!" Lord Fitzwilliam said indignantly as Lady Landsdown paled. "No, I am off immediately. Formsby? Do you accompany me?"

Lord Formsby looked up in consternation. He wished to remain at Lady Cecelia's side, but duty demanded otherwise.

"Of course. Help in any way I can," he said, reluctantly releasing Cecelia's hand.

The two men found pistols in Edward's study and loaded them as they waited for two horses to be brought around, for they had both arrived at Landsdown House in carriages. After what seemed like an eternity, the horses appeared. With urgent shouts of farewell, both men rushed out the front door. Suddenly Lord Fitzwilliam stopped and stared at the street, with the unfortunate result that Formsby crashed into him from behind at full tilt.

As the two men struggled to keep their balance, Samantha

calmly looked up from where she stood near the hackney cab.

"Please, my lord," she said quietly to Fitzwilliam. "Could you pay the driver?"

Then she walked past them into the house.

Chapter 16

As far as anyone could tell, Samantha was unharmed by her ordeal, although she seemed exceedingly reluctant to discuss the topic. Lady Landsdown was for alerting the watch as well as Samantha's mother, but Samantha merely said that it was not necessary as her captor had been a well-meaning but misguided person who regretted the abduction almost immediately and did everything possible to assure her safe arrival at Landsdown House.

Lord Fitzwilliam professed himself most unsatisfied by that explanation and vowed to wait for Edward's return to pursue the matter further, but when several hours passed without any sign of the earl, Fitz finally gave up and left in a huff.

As Cecelia very naturally wished to assure herself of Samantha's well-being, Lord Formsby reluctantly took himself off to allow the ladies to be reunited. He was much shaken by the evening's events, however, and the sudden realization that he could not rest until he could claim the responsibility and privilege of protecting Cecelia in his own right. And so it was a very pensive Lord Formsby whom Edward startled by his appearance that night at White's.

"Good God, Edward! Might have thought you would be at home with the ladies after what has happened! Or haven't you heard?" Formsby said in shocked surprise.

Edward settled into a comfortable brown leather chair and stretched out his long legs. His face was solemn, and there were faint lines that might have signaled fatigue. He rubbed one of his hands gingerly before returning his attention to his friend.

"Yes, there was quite a furor. The house was in a state when I arrived home, so much so that I was happy to take myself off again," he said quietly.

Formsby stared, dumbfounded.

"Never say you have done nothing to help Miss Compton?" he asked in astonishment.

"Nothing to be done. She claims to be unharmed, and I cannot think that it will serve to set Bow Street on a fellow whom no one can describe and who is likely halfway to Scotland by now."

Edward turned to catch a waiter's eye. Formsby threw him a disgusted look.

"I must say, Edward, I cannot approve of your cavalier treatment of this matter. The ladies might have been truly harmed. Why, your sister was nearly hysterical with fear! Took me nearly an hour to calm her!"

"Cecelia is made of strong stuff. I expect she will recover," Edward said dismissively and ordered a bottle of port. "Will you join me?" he added politely. "Although I can see you are in a fair way to making your way through your own bottle."

This was too much for Formsby, who stood indignantly.

"I collect I have been in grave misapprehension of your character these many years, Landsdown. Anyone who would treat such a horrifying ordeal so casually deserves the strongest censure!"

Edward looked up at Formsby, whose normally friendly brown eyes were cold and disapproving. The earl drained his glass. Abruptly his face darkened.

"Sit down, Henry. We have much to discuss," he ordered coolly. "Your conscience is not so blameless as your easy and presumptuous condemnation of my apparent sins suggests. It is time, my friend, to make your own accounting. First, I wish to hear about Blackwood and Samantha at the pits. And then you may explain your attentions to my sister.''

Formsby blanched, and his eyes looked away from Edward's uncompromising features. Finally he took his seat, deciding to pour himself another glass of port after all.

There followed during the next quarter hour a most informative confession, the earl learning as much as he suspected about Blackwood's nefarious attempt on Samantha and venting his fury at the fact that such an episode was not revealed to him.

"'Twas Miss Compton's wish to keep the lid on, but nothing could have persuaded me to, at least until you nearly accused me of trying to seduce her,'' Formsby insisted, his face flushed in awareness of the obvious lameness of the excuse. "Offended me that you would think such a thing. Let that color my judgment, I suppose. Ought to have told you anyway, but my mind has been occupied with other matters.''

"Indeed,'' Edward replied sternly. "That brings me to the topic of my sister. What game are you about, Henry? I gather that I was mistaken in believing all the attention you have paid her was to divert me from your designs on Samantha. Can it be that you are courting my sister in earnest?''

The blush that now suffused Formsby's face provided the answer, and Edward found himself smiling for the first time that night.

"What does my sister have to say about your efforts?'' he persisted, but Formsby slumped in his chair in apparent dejection.

"She thinks I am pretending to court her to throw you off the scent,'' Formsby said glumly.

At Edward's perplexed frown, he continued. "The idea was to have you think that I was interested in her so that you wouldn't force her to marry Fitz.''

"Fitz! But where did you get such a queer notion?''

''Why, from Lady Cecelia,'' the other returned.

Edward looked at him oddly. ''But Fitz is betrothed to Sam, didn't you know?''

Formsby stared, flabbergasted. ''Betrothed?'' he said blankly.

''Well, it was to remain secret until the masquerade, but I assumed Cecelia would have told you,'' Edward said, watching Formsby's reaction with interest.

That gentleman fell mute.

''The fact that she did not is interesting,'' Edward added thoughtfully. ''I suspect there is more here than meets the eye. I would not be surprised if those two young ladies were up to something.''

Lord Formsby was much struck by the news Edward had imparted, not a little puzzled, and not especially pleased with this turn of events. He mulled the matter over for some moments before recalling himself to his surroundings. Then, as the silence drew on, he glanced at Edward. The latter was rubbing his temples and appeared to be studying the tip of his boot. But he wore a faraway and preoccupied expression.

''And what about you, Edward?'' Formsby said. ''Unless I miss my mark, there is something else afoot. What deep game are you playing, my friend?''

Edward swirled the liquid around in his glass and took another swallow. He forced a smile, but it quickly faded.

''One with very high stakes,'' he admitted somberly, and then drained the glass.

The house was in a turmoil of planning for Lady Landsdown's masquerade, which was to take place in two days. The servants were polishing the oak, scouring the marble, and shining the glided frames so that the legions of Landsdown ancestors inside them would show to best advantage.

Each of the ladies in the house was, in her own way, at wit's end. Lady Landsdown, worrying that all would not be in readiness, dashed from room to room with instructions, making dozens of lists with tasks yet remaining to be accomplished. Cecelia was exceedingly distressed because Lord Formsby had not called upon her in the four days since their harrowing adventure with the highwayman. Nor had she run into him at any social events. She was constantly rushing into Samantha's chamber for anguished discussion of the possibilities.

"Do you think something has happened to him, Samantha? But surely Edward would have mentioned it," she said, wringing her handkerchief. "What can be wrong? I had begun to think that he had come to care for me."

And with that, she bit her lip in an effort to hold back tears.

Samantha forced her attention away from her own very distressing thoughts. Beholding her beautiful friend's tremulous countenance, she lost patience altogether.

"Stop it, Cecelia! There is no excuse for falling to pieces just because you have tumbled into love with the one man who did not cast himself at your feet!" she cried. "You are driving me mad! I can hardly think myself, so I do not know how you expect me to fathom the impenetrable brain of Lord Formsby!"

There was a long silence as Cecelia, quite taken aback, stood rigidly. Then she walked to Samantha's side and placed a hand on her shoulder.

"How selfish of me, Samantha! I had quite forgotten your recent ordeal! I had no right to thrust my silly troubles on you when you are so preoccupied," she said softly.

Samantha immediately regretted her words and gave Cecelia a bracing hug. "No, it is I who am being selfish," she said. "In truth, what with everything else, I had not given Lord Formsby a thought. But now that you remark upon it, his disappearance is a bit of a mystery. Might you not simply ask Edward? No, of course that would not do."

Samantha broke off and, picking up a quill on her writing desk, began to nibble it thoughtfully. "You have not had words?" she asked.

"Oh, no! When last we spoke, he was comforting me after your abduction. He was the soul of concern. Oh, Samantha! What if he has taken me in dislike?"

"Nonsense. I would wager my mother's pearls that Lord Formsby has been smitten since the first time he saw you. It must be something else." Samantha paused as a thought occurred to her. "You don't suppose, Cecelia, that he found out about Fitz?"

Cecelia blanched. "And realized I had tricked him? Never say so!" she exclaimed. "Oh, I am mortified, Samantha! He will think I played him for the veriest fool!"

"Well, he would have found out about the betrothal at all events at the masquerade," Samantha said practically.

Cecelia pulled at the handkerchief, in her distress tearing a small corner of the delicate linen.

"Yes, but I had hoped to manage a declaration from him by then! And now I do not know what to do! What if I should never see him again?" she cried.

Samantha frowned in disgust.

"Cecelia, you are becoming a silly watering pot! I know you for a woman of more sense. There is only one way out of this problem."

Cecelia looked up hopefully. "What is that?" she asked.

"Why, the direct approach," Samantha said briskly. "You must confess the whole of it to him, and throw yourself on his mercy! Tell him you plotted the entire scheme because you could not bear to live without him! He will be immensely flattered."

Cecelia gasped. "I cannot!"

"Well, then you must resign yourself to living without him," she said firmly, as Cecelia dissolved into tears.

"Stop it!" Samantha fairly shouted. "It will not be that difficult to pull off. You can intercept him at the ball if he has not come round by then. He has not sent his regrets, by any chance?"

Cecelia shook her head.

"Well, we can be thankful at least for that. There. 'Tis settled," Samantha said with a note of finality.

At Cecelia's look of dismay, she softened her tone. "I know it seems hard, but you have the mettle to manage it, Cecelia. There is little else to be done, at all events, not if you wish to persuade him you did not intend to make sport of him. I'll warrant he will be delighted when he understands that your motives arose from love.''

It was too bad, Samantha thought later, that she had no one to take her worries to—and a pity that she could not take her own advice and muster the courage to likewise confront Edward. But while she was sure that Lord Formsby was in love with Cecelia and could be brought around, she thought that Edward would be utterly appalled at such a declaration. Moreover, there was the strange and unsettling matter of the highwayman, whose sudden appearance in her life had turned her feelings all topsy-turvy. He had opened the door to sensations that had surpassed her wild imaginings. She thought about him night and day—when she was not thinking about Edward, that is. In fact, her feelings about him seemed all mixed up with her feelings about Edward. How could that be? Was she a complete wanton that her passions could be moved to such extremes by *two* men? She felt torn and confused, and her distress was deepened because there was no one she could turn to.

At one time, she might have turned to Edward. But he had questioned her only perfunctorily after the incident and since then had made himself so scarce that she had wondered if he was avoiding her. His lack of interest in her harrowing adventure provided eloquent testimony of his indifference. Indeed, he had shown only the merest curiosity about her ordeal.

''Would you be able to identify him, do you think?'' he had asked nonchalantly.

''No. At least . . .'' she began. ''It was dark, and he wore a mask and cloak. I do know that he was tall, and his hair was black, but I am not so certain it was his own, now that I think on it.''

He showed particular interest in that, but when she could provide no further details, he seemed bored and inclined to drop the matter altogether. He did not so much as look her way during most of their interview. She left feeling hurt and confused.

But in the midst of her confusion, there was one thing about which she now was certain. She could not marry Lord

Fitzwilliam. She had come to that stark realization despite
her painfully clear understanding of the duty and need to
secure her future. Under other circumstances, she might
have fallen in love with Lord Fitzwilliam. But now, knowing her sentiments toward Edward (and having experienced
such a strange and embarrassing intensity of feelings with a
complete stranger!), she could not settle for a marriage
whose chief recommendation seemed to be that the two
parties could converse at length quite amiably. And while
Lord Fitzwilliam set the pulses of many ladies racing,
Samantha knew with regret that he would never move her
that way.

Thus did her practical nature lose in the battle with
another, less familiar side. But in abandoning the security
Lord Fitzwilliam offered, Samantha knew she was dooming
herself to a life unwed. For her, there would be no other
Season. Still, she felt a measure of peace at her decision.
Somehow she would provide for her mother. But she could
not sacrifice her heart in the process.

The masquerade was a fitting finale to the Season, all that
Lady Landsdown had hoped it would be, and much more
besides.

The great ballroom had been hung for the occasion with
yellow damask festoons tied here and there with wide bands
of purple ribbon. The buffets exhibited much of the Landsdown collection of wrought plate, cups, vases, and ewers of
solid gold. Candelabra of silver gilt graced the mantel-
pieces, and the enormous crystal chandeliers shone on a
festive throng attired in various costumes of the past. The
guests danced and ate and glittered in the candlelight in a
bittersweet tribute to the dying Season. Perhaps the only
group who did not contribute their wholehearted enjoyment
to the evening were those young ladies whose futures were
not yet settled—and two of those number resided at Landsdown House.

Cecelia had chosen the Gothic costume of a twelfth-
century princess, and her elegant scarlet robe and long train
dragged on the ground as she moved. A thin silk veil

covered her face and imparted an air of mysteriousness. The modest head covering did not, however, quite offset the rather startling decolletage of her gown, which was cut straight across and very low on her breasts, far lower, in fact, than was generally considered quite the thing for an unmarried young lady. The startling effect of this costume was by design, a somewhat desperate effort on behalf of that beautiful young lady to use her considerable assets in the daunting task of securing Lord Formsby's affections. If the guests wondered at Lady Landsdown's acquiescence in her daughter's choice of costume, they did not voice their questions and would likely have been startled to see that the gown had provoked in the countess an expression more of amusement than anything else.

Samantha, in a moment of wistful nostalgia for the excursion with Edward to the Elgin Marbles, had created for herself a loosely draped garment typical of classical Greece and rather boldly patterned after the drapery the Fates had worn in the sculpture they had seen. The pale cream fabric fell simply and gracefully over one shoulder—the other being left bare—and was belted with shimmering golden bands under the breast and around the waist. Her chestnut hair was piled loosely upon her head, a single gold headband the only ornament. She did not set out to impersonate a Grecian goddess, only to pay tribute to that special visit; but those confronted with her beauty and her determined mien had the image of Athena immediately called to mind.

Heads turned when they passed, but the young ladies failed to notice. Cecelia was searching desperately for Lord Formsby in hopes of setting things aright. Samantha was looking for three gentlemen, but had so far failed to find any of them, causing her no small anxiety. The length and intensity of the deliberations that led to her resolve to end her betrothal had unfortunately left her no time to impart that decision to Lord Fitzwilliam; therefore Samantha was anxiously seeking that gentleman in order to head off his betrothal announcement. She was also looking for Edward, whom she had not seen at all that day, to tell him of her decision. Finally there was the matter of the highwayman, who had promised to appear in a black domino. Though she had only half believed it, she still searched the crowd for him.

Unfortunately there were dozens of black dominos, and for that matter, she had no idea what Lord Fitzwilliam or Edward would be wearing. In frustration, she leaned against an arch support at the rear of the ballroom. One of Edward's ancestors, elaborately framed above the mantelpiece, seemed to be smirking at her. Samantha sighed. This Season had not precisely turned out as she had planned.

"Miss?"

Samantha looked up at the servant at her elbow.

"Yes?"

"There's a gentleman looking for you. Told me to give you this," he said and, bowing, handed her a note on a silver salver.

Samantha took the missive and opened it, her eyes widening as she read the inscription: *I must see you at once on a matter of extreme urgency!* It was unsigned.

"Who sent this?" she demanded.

"Didn't give his name, miss, but he is waiting just outside the door over yonder," the servant said and gestured to a door leading off a hallway that ran the alley side of the house.

Samantha frowned, then had a thought.

"This man," she asked anxiously, "how was he dressed?"

"In black he was, miss. That's about all I could see."

Samantha's brow cleared.

"Take me to him," she ordered.

He was here! Her pulse raced as she went through the door to him. He stood in the alley, a shadow blending into the blackness of the night. She moved toward him, extending her hand hesitantly.

"You came," she said simply.

There was a momentary silence, then an unpleasant chuckle.

"But, of course, Miss Compton. Nothing could keep me away."

Samantha gasped at the velvety voice. Blackwood!

But before she could react, he had thrown a cape over her and hustled her into the waiting carriage. She struggled under its folds, but it was a brief and futile effort. Suddenly she suffered a painful blow, and all went dark.

Cecelia was studying the monk who had just bowed rather stiffly and requested the next dance. Although his face was masked except for his mouth, she recognized the brown eyes that held hers with a rather inscrutable expression. Moreover, she felt a tingling sensation that she knew unerringly arose from his presence.

"Lord Formsby?" she asked tentatively.

The figure inclined his head stiffly but declined to answer. Instead, he offered his hand as the orchestra struck up a waltz. They danced in silence, Cecelia holding her train with one hand as she executed the steps. She tripped once on its cumbersome folds, but a strong arm steadied her and, she might have imagined, held her somewhat closer after that. When the dance ended, he bowed again and would have released her, but she touched the sleeve of his brown robe.

"Pray, wait, Sir Monk. I do not know your identity, but you remind me very much of a dear acquaintance I have not seen in some time," she said, and there was a note of pleading in her voice. "Say you will stay and bear me company?"

The figure hesitated. He appeared to be studying her closely. His eyes traveled down her face to the deep neckline of her gown before he averted them hurriedly. In resignation, she started to move away, but his hand quickly reached out to stop her. He extended his arm, and they walked in the direction of the courtyard.

"I am afraid that this friend may be terribly angry with me," Cecelia began hesitantly, unused to the role of penitent but determined to plunge ahead. "You see, I wasn't entirely truthful, and I believe he thinks I meant to make sport of him."

The figure cleared his throat but did not speak.

"If I could but find him, I would explain that I only sought occasions to spend time in his company and perhaps earn his good opinion," she said, looking up shyly.

The monk remained silent, and she continued resolutely: "If truth be told, Sir Monk, I wished to make him fall in love with me. You see, I did not think he cared."

As they entered the courtyard, he stopped and turned to face her. He seemed about to speak, but her finger gently touched his mouth. Taking a deep breath, she rushed on.

"The tragedy, Sir Monk, is that I fear I have given him a thorough disgust of me. And I do not think I can bear it! For he is quite the world to me. I have loved him for the longest time, and yet I never told him. Do you think somehow I can let him know?" She looked up into a pair of troubled brown eyes.

The monk seemed to consider this question for a moment. Cecelia waited, afraid to breathe. Then he spoke.

"Perhaps I can deliver your message, my lady, although it may be . . . difficult," he said formally.

Her face fell. Then, with a smile that transformed his solemn features, he added: "Probably take a kiss to persuade a chucklehead like that."

Radiant, Cecelia lifted her face to his.

"Got to do something about that veil, though," the monk added, frowning, and showed her what he meant.

He saw her in the corner across the room. It took ten minutes to make his way through the crowd, and he was relieved to see the Grecian-clad figure was still there. How like her to wear such a costume, he thought with a smile. Then he took a deep breath. He might be making the biggest fool of himself, but he had to take that risk. He would tell her tonight.

Edward placed his hand on her shoulder and slowly, almost as if she had expected him, she turned. He froze when he saw her face.

"Hello, Edward," said Lady Darrow. Her smile was one of triumph.

* * *

Samantha's head ached, and her wrists were rubbed raw by the length of rope that bound them behind her back. She had no notion where she was, only that the location did not seem far from town. She sat in a wooden chair in a room with the barest pretense of furniture. A candle illuminated her captor's face. He took off his coat and threw it on the nearby table.

"Pity that none of your well-bred friends are around to rescue you now. But I fear no one knows of this tiny hunting box," said the velvet voice, exuding mock pity.

Samantha blocked the fear from her mind and looked at him in disgust.

"On the contrary, Lord Blackwood, it is a pity that I was ever so green as to believe that you had some shred of decency in you," she snapped.

He threw back his head and laughed.

"Ah, yes. The rake waiting for reformation into a paragon at the hands and heart of an innocent young lady," he said. At her look of surprise, he laughed. "I have heard it before. You ladies seem to have your heads filled with such nonsense. Everyone seems intent on reforming me. They fail to see I have no wish for it or that it cannot be done."

He moved closer, his face so near that she could feel his breath on her neck.

"You see, Miss Compton—or may I call you Samantha, since we are soon to be on such intimate terms—I have no use for such silly games. I really am thoroughly unacceptable, you know, although my title and wealth go far in overcoming the scruples of those respectable arbiters of propriety. When gentlemen lose their last guinea to Captain Sharp, for instance, I am their dearest friend. The ladies play an entirely different game, you understand. They scorn me in their ballrooms but find me a most pleasant companion in their bedchambers."

Samantha recoiled, but Blackwood merely trailed his hand lightly down one of her arms and up her side. She felt as though she were going to be ill.

"As for you, my innocent, since your fortune—or rather

lack of it—requires you to sell yourself to the highest bidder, I am only simplifying your choice. Indeed, I am more than willing to part with some small funds to increase your enjoyment of my company. And who's to say? Perhaps you will have more success at reforming me than your predecessors. For I will give you this, Miss Compton: you are a most unusual lady.''

His fingertip moved along her bare shoulder and slid across to the other, where he hooked his finger under the thin silk of her Grecian costume. Quite nonchalantly, he pulled the fabric down, leaving both shoulders bare and the top of her breasts exposed.

Blackwood smiled and began to caress the creamy skin. Samantha cringed and closed her eyes. She tried to block out the room, its sights, sounds, and smells, for she knew that was the only hope for survival. Therefore, she did not immediately realize that another voice was speaking.

''Apparently you did not take my earlier warning to heart, Blackwood,'' said a honeyed baritone. ''I regret that I was not able to make myself perfectly clear.''

Blackwood whirled and was instantly arrested at the sight of the pistol pointing at his chest. Lord Landsdown stood silhouetted in the doorway in a flowing black cloak like some avenging specter. Behind him was Lord Fitzwilliam, but Blackwood's eyes were riveted on the former, who was speaking again.

''However,'' the earl continued, his voice now cold and hard, ''I trust that this time there will be no mistake.''

The cobalt eyes were suffused with such steely anger that, involuntarily, the marquess looked away. Only then did Edward's eyes seek Samantha, who was staring in amazed relief.

''You are unharmed.'' His question was delivered in the flat tones of a statement willed to be fact.

''Yes,'' she said quietly. Without a flicker of acknowledgment, the earl returned his gaze to Blackwood.

''It is a great temptation to shoot you on the spot, Blackwood, although I would much rather see you dance in the hangman's noose.''

The marquess remained silent.

"Unfortunately," Edward continued, "a public trial and hanging would damage this lady's reputation, so our only solution to this distasteful business seems to be a quiet and speedy transportation. And that, I swear before God, will be arranged before the sun rises."

The knowledge that he was beaten did not prevent an unpleasant smile from crossing Blackwood's face. Finally he found his tongue.

"It seems you have won this round, Landsdown, the beneficiary, I gather, of Catharine's . . . good offices," he said. "Alas, even I failed to anticipate that a woman will go to such extraordinary lengths for her lover."

Samantha blanched, and she saw Edward's eyes flick briefly in her direction before returning without emotion to Blackwood.

"On the contrary, Blackwood. It was indeed Lady Darrow who informed me of your plans and location, but I can assure you it was not an altogether voluntary effort on her part," Edward said grimly. "And now, if you please, you will accompany me on a brief journey."

In the space of the next few moments, Samantha found herself bundled into a carriage for the return trip to town, Lord Fitzwilliam at her side. Edward had vanished. It was left to Fitzwilliam to explain, as he tucked a blanket around Samantha, that Edward was taking her abductor to a place where he would be swiftly transported with few questions asked.

"Though such a fate is too good for him," Fitzwilliam added angrily as they rolled toward town. "It is well past time for putting an end to that one."

He clasped her hand reassuringly and chatted away, but Samantha heard none of his words. Her mind was riveted on the picture of Edward as he confronted Blackwood, his hard anger penetrating her dazed distress and banishing forever any lingering image of her cherished childhood playmate. The awkward but vulnerable boy who had gallantly rescued her by dashing pepper on the hounds had vanished forever. In his stead was a man whose heart was so hardened that he could spare barely a glance for a woman he had known most of his life.

And what of Lady Darrow? Samantha's dazed mind had heard only that she owed her rescue to that lady, which confirmed her worst fears. Edward and Lady Darrow were lovers, for how else would Edward discover Blackwood's plans?

No longer could she avoid facing facts. Her spirits, which should have been elated at her deliverance, sunk to a new low. Now she saw the harsh reality of the side of Edward that kept the world at arm's length. That cold image he presented to society now seemed very much a part of him. He had not let down his guard for an instant to commiserate with her plight, nor had he endeavored to assure himself privately of her well-being. He had simply vanished with his prisoner. Where was her friend and confidant?

In despair, she could not stifle a small sob.

At length, she realized that Lord Fitzwilliam was staring at her and that she did not know how long it had been since he stopped talking. She looked at him in embarrassment.

"What is it, Samantha?" he asked softly.

She gave him a look of apology. "I cannot marry you, my lord," she said sadly. "I am terribly sorry."

"I know."

Samantha looked over at him in surprise. "What?"

He sighed and squeezed her hand. "You are in love with Edward."

Samantha blushed. "How did you know?" she asked in a whisper.

He kissed her hand softly. "I saw your face back there," he said quietly. "It was quite a simple deduction."

Samantha leaned back against the cushions.

"I am terribly sorry, my lord," she said, and closed her eyes against the tears that had suddenly made vision impossible.

Chapter 17

Juliana stared at Edgedown, whose face bore a look of appalled horror.

"You what?" he asked, aghast.

"I have fallen in love with you." Juliana turned away, unable to bear the pity in his eyes. She pulled out her handkerchief and wept loudly.

There was an awful silence from Edgedown as he groped for a response. Finally he took her hand.

"You know that I have always cared for you, Juliana," he said earnestly, "but my affection arises from the bonds of friendship and not any other cause. I am deeply sorry if I have given you reason to think otherwise."

He looked at her with an air of uncertainty that bordered on distaste.

"I think it would be wise to escort you home now," he said, and turned toward the door.

But to his mortification Juliana threw herself at his departing figure, in her clumsiness managing to grasp only one of his legs. They both tumbled to the ground and she heard a crashing sound. He stared in horror as his mother's ancient oriental vase shattered into hundreds of tiny pieces.

"That was priceless!" he shouted.
"Not as priceless as our love!" she cried, and clung
tightly to his magnificently polished boot.

Samantha picked up the manuscript and flung the pages
into the fire. She had come to thoroughly despise Juliana.
Edgedown was proving himself no prize, either. She wished
the whole lot of them at the devil. That she had been able to
create such a pack of ne'er-do-wells could only be attributed
to the strange madness that had completely taken over her
brain.

That could be laid firmly at Edward's door, but if she did
not have a care, she would meet Juliana's ignominious fate.

No. She would never sink that low. Or could she? She
had marched nearly in lockstep with Juliana—from her silly
infatuation with an incorrigible rake to her misguided
betrothal and her unrequited love for a childhood friend.
Was there any remaining vestige of sanity to prevent her
from racing into Edward's study, declaring her love, and
casting herself at his feet like an utter fool?

Samantha shuddered. Edward had not yet returned from
disposing of Blackwood. She was very much afraid that
when he did, he would remain that forbiddingly aloof man
who had freed her from the marquess's clutches but left her
heart trembling with his cold rejection. No, there seemed to
be no hope except to continue on as friends. But was
keeping Edward's friendship worth the price of never
declaring her love?

Samantha wandered over to her window. She could see
Lord Formsby and Cecelia sitting close together in the
courtyard below, looking thoroughly besotted. At least
something had resolved itself favorably.

Dejected, she abandoned the empty sanctuary of her room
and wandered aimlessly down the corridor. When her feet
stopped at the door of Lady Landsdown's sitting room, she
raised her hand and knocked hesitantly.

"Come in," that lady said, and Samantha pushed open
the door.

Lady Landsdown surveyed Samantha's troubled face.

She did not think that it was caused by last night's episode, as harrowing and distressing as it had been. The countess was now very much awake to the undercurrents preoccupying certain of the residents of Landsdown House. She poured tea for both of them.

"You know, Samantha, I promised your mother to look after you and do everything I can to secure your future. And yet I seemed to have failed on both accounts," Lady Landsdown began.

Samantha opened her mouth to protest, but Lady Landsdown shook her head and continued.

"But you need not look so depressed, my dear. Blackwood will never trouble you again," she said reassuringly. "The Season is ending, but I have a strong sense that we will find a husband for you yet."

Samantha frowned in dismay.

"Oh, but Lady Landsdown, you must not blame yourself for the events of last night! It was my own foolishness that put me in such a pickle! As for Lord Fitzwilliam, well, he was most understanding. That was also my fault, for I discovered belatedly that I could not marry where my heart was not engaged."

Lady Landsdown peered at Samantha over her teacup.

"Then I collect, my dear, that your heart *is* engaged elsewhere? I do not see how you could have come to such a conclusion otherwise."

Samantha's face reddened, and she suddenly felt completely tongue-tied. Lady Landsdown reached over and patted her hand.

"Forgive my boldness, Samantha, but the happiness of those close to me is of utmost importance."

Samantha was not certain she understood the countess's statement. But she knew she had to speak to someone.

"There *is* someone, Lady Landsdown, only we are but friends, and I despair of him considering me otherwise. But if I tell him the truth, I am desperately afraid of losing his friendship, which is of utmost importance to me!"

Lady Landsdown cocked her head thoughtfully. "More important than love?" she asked softly.

Samantha was silent as she considered. ''No, I suppose not. Only, well, I risk everything, do I not?''

''And nothing,'' came the enigmatic response.

Samantha stared at Lady Landsdown in confusion.

''That is not all, I'm afraid,'' Samantha continued after a moment. ''I had always discounted the rather . . . aloof image that he presented to the world because our discourse had been marked by warmth and affection. But now I see that I was mistaken. It seems he has no use for a love like mine. He has built a wall around his heart, and I fear it cannot be scaled.''

''And just how do you know that?''

''Well,'' Samantha conceded, ''there were times when it did seem as if he wished for more than friendship, not to diminish that inestimable and valued state, of course . . .''

''Of course,'' murmured her ladyship.

''. . . but I fear that perception came from my overactive imagination,'' she said, tossing her hands up in despair. ''Truly, I do not think that he has a passionate bone in his body!''

Lady Landsdown threw back her head and laughed. ''And I think, Samantha Compton, that you are very, very wrong!''

Samantha's confusion was now complete, and as she stared at Lady Landsdown in utter perplexity, she became aware of footsteps in the hallway. The door opened, and Edward stood there. He appeared exhausted and still wore remnants of his attire from the previous night's masquerade.

Still, Samantha thought as she took in the lines of fatigue and the windswept blond hair, his presence was as commanding as it had been when he stood in Blackwood's doorway in his black domino. And while he had since discarded the cloak, Samantha could not but admire the way he still showed to advantage in the black shirt and pantaloons he had worn underneath. Despite his fatigue, he had never looked more magnificent.

Except once, said an urgent voice in her head.

The black domino! She gasped and sat bolt upright. Her

mind's eye brought forth the image of a highwayman towering over his captive in a tiny cottage, pinning her with his body and kissing her into longing submission. Surely that passionate rogue could not be Edward! But every instinct now told her that he was! Had he not worn the black domino?

Lady Landsdown and Edward were looking at her strangely, and Samantha realized in chagrin that the tiny shriek she had just heard had come from her own mouth.

"Are you well, Sam?" Edward asked, frowning.

Samantha found that she could not speak. Instead, she began to laugh uncontrollably. Her teacup rattled noisily, and Lady Landsdown calmly reached over and took it from her hand.

"I believe Samantha is still suffering from the effects of last night's ordeal," she said serenely, turning to Edward. "Welcome home, dear. But do take yourself off and make yourself more presentable."

The earl eyed the two women doubtfully, but finally turned on his heel and quit the room.

"Now, dear, you must tell me everything," Lady Landsdown insisted.

Samantha looked across the tea table, her hazel eyes shining with a spark that had not been there moments before.

"Lady Landsdown," she began, wiping away the tears of laughter, "I do believe I need your assistance."

Lord Landsdown sat brooding in his study, a glass of Madeira in his hand. He had changed his travel-stained clothes for a superbly cut coat of bottle green, a pair of buff trousers, and perfectly polished brown boots. His cravat was flawless, having been achieved in only one try, despite the earl's exhausted state. And despite the fatigue evident in his face, his cobalt eyes radiated a pent-up energy that bespoke his growing frustration.

The problem of Samantha Compton was very much with him. It had occupied his brain throughout the long ride

home. It so consumed him that he could not wait to see her
and had consequently elected not to stop for the night at an
inn. But now that he was here, he felt like a complete fool.
What had he been about with this ridiculous plan of his?
Long weeks of plotting to insinuate himself into her heart,
that absurd abduction in a highwayman's disguise and that
dreadful wig—where had it all led? He had not been able
to shield her from that miscreant Blackwood. And while
last night's villainy may have delayed Samantha's betrothal
announcement, Edward had no doubt that one would soon
be forthcoming. Worst of all, her first reaction today upon
seeing him, her rescuer, was that of uncontrollable laughter!
His dejection was complete, his sense of failure absolute.

And yet, perversely, he found that he could not let her go,
even to save his valued sense of pride. Having once thrown
caution to the wind, he seemed unable to do otherwise. For
once in his life he had risked everything and had found the
experience oddly exhilarating. Edward sighed. His life was
becoming something out of Sam's books. But so be it. He
could not forget the abject terror he had felt upon seeing her
at Blackwood's mercy. It had taken every ounce of his
control not to race to her side. Well, if he must play the fool,
he must. He would be damned if she would marry anyone
else, even if he had to carry her kicking and screaming to the
altar. He tossed back the rest of the glass. With an air of
determination, he rose.

A knock on the door arrested his progress. Sam? But no,
it was merely Petersham with the strange announcement
that his coach waited out front.

"I did not order a carriage, Petersham," the earl said in
irritation.

"Nevertheless, my lord, one awaits," was the patient
reply.

"Well, send it away, man!" Edward said testily.

"Begging your pardon, my lord, but Miss Compton said
it was your express wish to go driving with her this
afternoon. I believe she also voiced the hope that you would
not keep her waiting."

"What the devil?" Edward demanded, and marched

down the hall to the front door. He saw that his coach and four, an odd ensemble for a drive in the park, were indeed waiting.

"Miss Compton is within?" he asked in consternation.

"I believe so, my lord."

Edward abandoned all hope of making sense of this development and walked out to the carriage.

"Hello, Edward," Samantha said as she rapped to signal John Coachman.

The carriage lurched forward, and Edward reached out to steady himself as he took the seat next to her.

"What is this all about, Sam?" he demanded, but she merely returned a look of bland innocence.

"Why, I am abducting you, Edward," she replied in her most offhand manner.

"You are *what?*" He stared at her, flabbergasted.

"Do not worry, for I shall not harm you. But you might have a care for those nice clothes of yours. The road past Paddington is rather dusty, I'm afraid," she said apologetically.

He stared at her.

"This is nonsense!" he thundered. But he found that when he tried to order John to stop, that individual had suddenly become quite deaf.

"You see, Edward? I'm afraid you are most definitely at my mercy," Samantha said calmly.

Edward sat back on the seat and crossed his arms. She detected a dangerous expression in his eyes, but his tone was quite civil.

"Very well, then," he said with elaborate politeness. "May I ask where you are taking me?"

"You shall see," was the only response.

They drove in silence for some time, and Samantha felt her senses tingle with the force of his gaze. But he did not speak.

She was relieved when she felt the carriage leave the main road. Edward, she saw, was looking out the window with a vaguely puzzled air. Suddenly his brow cleared, and he turned to her with a burning expression.

"How did you know about this place?" he demanded.

His question went unanswered as the carriage rolled to a stop in front of the tiny hut. Samantha gestured to the steps the coachman had quickly let down.

"I cannot exit until you do, sir," she said pointedly to Edward.

He frowned and stepped out, turning to help her. But when he would have released her hand, she would not allow it. He looked at her questioningly, but she merely pulled him toward the cottage and through the entrance as the sounds of his departing coach reached his ears.

"Now you will tell me what this is all about," he commanded softly, and the menacing edge in his voice made Samantha's pulse race.

"Certainly, Edward," she said sweetly and, parting her lips, lifted her face and boldly pressed them to his.

He gave a sharp, surprised intake of breath, and his arms came up in a halfhearted effort to resist. But by then his lips had begun to respond, and his protesting arms instead caught her waist and pressed her to him.

Suddenly something between them caught fire. Swiftly and fiercely their mouths sought deeper contact, and their burning bodies found their own intimate embrace. Consumed by sensations that had smoldered for too long, they ignited like a bed of dry leaves. For a long while, they lost all sense of time or place in the desperate urgency of a lover's embrace.

At last Edward released her, a strange and tormented look on his face. Samantha felt so weak that she would have fallen had he not reached out his arm to steady her.

"Yes, I have definitely found you out, Edward," she said in an unsteady voice. "Only, perhaps I had best be certain."

She raised her swollen lips to his, and he hesitated only a moment before taking them again. But finally he thrust himself from her.

"This is . . ." he began shakily.

"Most dangerous?" she offered helpfully. "But I am not yet ready to set you free, Edward. I wish to know about your dreams. The faces you see as you fall asleep at night, the ladies who enliven your nocturnal adventures."

His embarrassed smile and a deep red flush betrayed him. "You do know."

She nodded.

"Then you must know as well that there are no ladies in my dreams but you," he said simply.

"Although," he added after a moment's consideration, "I wonder whether that is indeed a proper description of the wanton I have encountered today."

Samantha smiled and nestled into his arms.

"Well, for that matter, sir, one who takes to the road as a highwayman to secure a lady's attentions is no gentleman, as I believe I once told you," she said.

"Nevertheless," she conceded with a devilish smile, "it was as masterfully done as anything my heroes ever managed."

"Except for a few . . . clumsy moments," Edward interjected, and she knew from his smile that he was thinking of his awkward tumble over the oaken bucket.

"I am sure it is the only time Lord Landsdown has displayed to less than perfect advantage," she said playfully.

In response, he pulled her tightly to him, his lips grazing her earlobe and sending goose bumps down her spine.

"How did you figure it out?"

"Oh, but I was a slowtop, Edward, or I would have managed it sooner. There was the black domino, of course, but I was too frightened and dazed at Blackwood's to put it all together last night. It was only today that I realized."

His brows drew together angrily at the mention of Blackwood's name.

"I wanted to kill him," he said. "If anything had happened to you, I could not have borne it."

She studied his tormented face. "I did not understand. You were so withdrawn, so aloof, so . . . *Landsdown*."

He colored guiltily.

"Have I been so stuffy as that?"

In answer, she lifted her face for a kiss. They continued that exercise for some moments until Edward suddenly remembered something.

"Fitz!" He looked at Samantha with stricken eyes.

"Understands completely and is no doubt breathing a sigh of relief at the knowledge that he does not have to marry such a hoyden," she responded softly, gently pulling his head downward so that they could resume their former exercise. Again the room was silent for some time.

"You never answered my question about how you discovered this place," he murmured finally.

Samantha smiled. "Your mother."

"My *mother?*"

"It seems she and your papa used this cottage as a favorite . . . retreat, and when I described it, she knew it instantly. She arranged everything."

He began to laugh, but suddenly Samantha had a disturbing thought.

"It's all right, isn't it Edward? I do treasure your friendship, only I wanted this more," she said earnestly. "I was afraid that you would take me in disgust if you knew that I loved you with all of my heart. Please say that it is all right."

His arms tightened around her.

"We shall always be the best of friends, my love," he said, caressing her hair. "But I, too, want this so very much."

She gave a sigh of contentment.

"I should have spoken earlier," he said. "But I was afraid you would be appalled at a declaration from one whom you regarded as a brother. I tried in my own way to bring you around to a different view, but I did not think I was very persuasive."

"Oh, but you were, Edward, you were," Samantha said, and the golden flecks in her hazel eyes radiated fires of happiness and passion.

He deposited a gentle kiss on her head. Then he stepped back to fix her with a stern gaze.

"Now may we put an end to all these abductions, Sam?" he asked with his best mock hauteur. "It is really bad *ton*."

A great whoop of laughter was the only response.